"The Hidden Church... ReVealed"

All New - (2nd edition)

By Loretta Askew Owens

Co-Editors:

Ian M. Flaherty, Loretta Askew Owens

and David Theodore

Visit:

www.*TheHiddenChurch.com*

**Published by
DNA eBooks Publishing Company
P.O. BOX 314
New York, NY 10037**

www.DNAeBooks.com

Publisher@DNAeBooks.com

ISBN - 978-0-9832476-4-7

DNA eBooks Publishing Company

DNA eBooks Publishing Group

"This Book is Dedicated to My Amazing, Wonderful Four Children: Robert, Enoch, Jacob and Sophia."

- GOD Bless, with Love Your Mother...

<u>Acknowledgements</u>:

*I would like to acknowledge "...The Writing Center at St. Cloud State University..." (Write Place) for the many hours spent helping to revise this book. I would like to give a Special Thanks to **Ian M. Flaherty** for making the book come ALIVE....*

Thank You Very Much for

Purchasing My eBook and

Thank You So Much for Supporting

all Our Authors and Writers:

Feel Free to Contact and Email Me:

Loretta@DNAeBooks.com

Visit – DNAeBooks.com
The Place to HangOut for all Reading Groups
and for all of Us who Enjoy Reading.

The DNA eBooks Publishing Group
Can Bring Authors / Writers to Your Events.
email us: Events@DNAeBooks.com

MEET OUR WRITERS and AUTHORS,
WATCH VIDEOS and MUCH MORE:

Check Out – DNAeBooks.com

Special Offers, Exclusive Content and More
Sign Up and be on Our VIP Email List
email us: VIPList@DNAeBooks.com

http://www.dnaebooks.com/short-form/
For information:
The DNA eBooks Publishing Group
P.O. BOX 314
New York City, NY 10037

"The Hidden Church… ReVealed"

(2nd edition)

By Loretta Askew Owens

Chapter 1

Sophie drove along the winding mountain road. She marveled at the beauty of the peaks; the grass was still green, and a patch of pink wild flowers was emerging from beneath a piece of driftwood in Yellowstone National Park. The foliage was in full bloom, though the snow now began to cover it. She was amazed as the snowflakes fell. Having started out on a clear day, the sky was now dark, and the temperature had dropped below freezing. The wind was howling as the visibility dimmed. The snowflakes were like hideous little faces bouncing off the windshield. She still thought that there was nothing more beautiful than a flower in the snow, but at the end of May, it was an unusual sight. When Sophie had left the cabin a half-hour ago, she had planned on attending a meeting high up in the mountains. Her family was still quite wealthy, and further pressure for religious consolidation was a necessary precaution, as well as a personal vendetta. The temperature at one moment had been 60 degrees; now it was 20.

It's good that this car has heat, she thought. She was wearing a thin, knee-length, sleeveless black dress underneath a spring coat. Yet, as she grew nervous, sweat began to pour from her forehead. The God thought was still in the back of Sophie's mind, and as she continued to drive, her mind flashed back to her nanny, Julia, who had practically raised her when she was young. Sophie could not forget for a moment the stories she heard from the woman when she was seven. Julia would tell her about a God who loved her and gave up the best part of Himself for that love, begetting a beloved Son with whom he was well pleased.

"This Son of God had to shed His blood for you Sophia," Julia said.

"Why did He have to bleed for me Julia?"

"Mortal man came from the Son of God called Adam." Julia had then paused and asked Sophie if she understood.

Sophie said, "Who was Adam?"

"He was the first man, and from him every human who was not begotten of fallen angels was of Adam."

"What are fallen angels Julia?"

"I'm not going to tell you that story today; maybe when you're older though."

While Sophie was thinking back to the stories Julia had told her, she realized Julia had never told the story of the fallen angels. Though Sophie no longer believed in God, the more she thought about Julia, the more her emotions were stirred up, and the more her disbelief came into question. As the weather got worse, fear of her intentions against Christians began to grip her. The snow was now sticking to the windshield, and no matter how fast the wipers were going, the snow just piled up until Sophie knew she needed to stop. However, there was no way to get out of the car; the snow was up to the windows on both sides. On the narrow roadway, there was now only one lane open for further traffic. Sophie was afraid that if she stopped completely, a car might come and wouldn't be able to see her, as the ferocious wind was creating a cloud of wet snow that made it almost impossible to see.

Yet, no matter how alone Sophie now felt, God had not abandoned her. As a part of His plan, He allowed this turbulence to continue in her life. He needed her to open her heart again before her world was completely torn apart. God wanted Sophie to reestablish who she was. In a world of hatred, bitterness, and pain, she would never realize the whole without Him. Until then, she would always be broken: a part disconnected from the whole. Without this original source, she would then never find her true purpose; without her true purpose, she would never find God's favor, as God finds displeasure in anything artificial and false. Even her name, Sophie, was not genuine. Her true name, Sophia, meant wisdom. Sophia's mother called her Sophie because she did not hear the Lord when He had first said her daughter's name. Her mother's human consciousness mistook it for Sophie. The Lord had been concerned about the mistaken name because of the power of the Word; the name Sophie was merely borrowed from the Greek name, Sophia. Since Sophie was derived from

Sophia, it would forever provide only a shadow of the definition of the original.

She must not prolong her time away from her mission, God thought, *and she can't delay it any longer, because the clock is ticking. Unless she becomes as wise as the meaning of her name, many souls will stay trapped in darkness.* He would not allow the God-thought escape Sophie's mind.

All of these things were going on in the mind of God as Sophie drove because He knew that she must wake up to what He had planned for her. Driving to her destination to ban the Christians from freedom of expression, the very thought of what Julia told her about the love of Jesus Christ was too painful to believe. Her hand crunched the wheel and sweat poured off her forehead as she fought her emotions. Sophie tried not to hate the memory from when she was seven, but it was too much when Julia left without saying goodbye. Not only did Sophie lose Julia, but the very Idea of Jesus Christ was snatched away from her. Julia had been like a mother to Sophie, and this loss instilled bitterness in her heart that would never go away. She had always given Sophie such warm hugs, something Sophie's mother and father never did. From somewhere deep inside, Julia had always felt that Sophie should be called *Sophia.* And after Julia left, whenever she heard the name Sophia, a warm feeling would cover her whole body. At the same time, pain often won over, because her hate was stronger than the memories of the love she felt for Julia.

Her mind then passed back into her early childhood with Julia; her hands begin to relax on the wheel. As she recalled the first time Julia used the name "Sophia" in front of her mother, Sophie remembered her mother's indignant tone and the arrogant look on her face.

"Do I call you another name?!" her mother had said. "I want you to call my daughter the name she was given at birth."

Sophie had started to laugh at how her mother commented on her name, but at same time she was glad that at least her mother wasn't willing to give it up. At that moment, Sophie felt a belonging that she'd never had with her mother before, even though their relationship was of no comparison to her relationship with Julia.

During Sophie's childhood, Jesus Christ had already been starting to lose popularity in the world. The reason for this was due to the Christians' refusal to meld with the other major religions, as the very doctrine of Christianity said that a redeemer was sent to bring the fallen creation back to the Father. Before Sophie had come to the decision to go into the mountains to essentially propose the genocide of Christians, the religious conflict had already started. Society was pushing for a one-world religion. The wars that took place involving religious differences had previously prevented agreements on how to deal with famine, water pollution, air pollution, terrorism, and overpopulation in the world. The future goal was to make a one-world government. It was important for society to ban Christianity because they, among others, had refused to become one with other religions. They were adamant in their belief that Jesus Christ was the only way to God. The Christians still had a strong hold on the world and it kept the people divided instead of supporting the one-world government.

During this time, Sophie's parents were held in high esteem in society because they had great investments in three of the most prosperous businesses in the country. They owned more than half of the businesses stock, giving them the power to run them as they pleased. Therefore, it was important how they conducted themselves in everyday life. Most people gave them respect by greeting them warmly to their faces, but behind their backs, most people despised them because they knew if they did not jump when her parents gave orders, they would lose their jobs. Her parents had so much power that even the present government had to watch how they treated the family. However, even though many people feared Sophie's family, Julia did not fear anyone but God. Julia knew she was walking on dangerous ground when she taught Sophie about Jesus Christ, but she just could not keep this good news from Sophie because she was like her own child.

Sophie's mother hired Julia six months before Sophie was born, both to help with the pregnancy, and to be a nanny to

10

Sophie. Her parents wanted an heir to their wealthy estate. Even though Sophie's mother agreed to have a child to please her husband, she resented the idea of any discomfort she had to endure for the course of the pregnancy.

Sophie's mother would say, "I will be glad when this baby is out of me."

In response, Julia would pat her stomach and say, "Oh don't feel bad sweetheart; your nanny love you."

Sophie's mother was never even fazed by this comment. Her face was like ice, showing no emotion. The baby angrily kicked when she felt the pain of rejection from her mother. As Julia stood in front of Sophie's mother, she was shocked when she saw a foot stretch the skin of her mother's belly and then back down slowly.

Julia reacted, shouting, "What was that!?"

"I guess the baby didn't like my coldness," she said in a calm voice.

Sophie's mother knew she would have to share the spotlight with the new baby and was afraid she would lose attention from her husband. The more Sophie's mother thought about the meaning of love, anxiety set in, which made her impatient, stressful, and extremely insecure.

Because she didn't understand love, she said in an indignant voice, "Just control yourself when the baby is born; I don't want to hear any more comments about love." When Sophie was born, she gazed at Julia as if she had known her forever; melting Julia's heart and bonding with her for the first 45 minutes that Sophie stared at her.

As Sophie drove, she thought about the story Julia had told her about when she was born; She felt a warm feeling come over her as she remembered Julia saying, "The first 45 minutes when you were born it was love at first sight."

Chapter 2

Sophie continued to drive along the treacherous roadway, though she was more relaxed now and began to think about the last time she saw Julia. Julia had been 26 years old and seemed so tall and beautiful to the seven-year old Sophie. Sophie had liked feeling Julia's soft lamb's wool hair as well as running her hand over the dark velvet complexion of her cheek. Since then, when Sophie went to bed with the soft wool blanket, she often thought of Julia's hair and what Julia said to her after she gave her the blanket. "Sophia, I want you to remember me every time you think about this blanket. If something ever happens where we can't be together, I want you to know I will always love you."

Whenever Sophie's mom and dad went on the town they would call Julia to watch Sophie. She remembered her parents being very punctual. They would leave in the evening and would return at 11 p.m. sharp. Whenever Sophie's parents would leave, Julia would get excited; she would show her snow-white teeth and smile because she could finally be herself, singing and praying freely. Once, when Julia sang, Sophie asked her who this Jesus was. At that time, Sophie was only three years old. Julia had paused for about 30 seconds with a hand on her chin, contemplating the consequence before she answered Sophie.

"Sophia, some people don't like this Jesus Christ, and I could get in trouble if I told you about Him. But, you can sing along with me if you like."

At first, it was like a game to Sophie; she would sing, "Tell me about what you're singing about; tell me what you're singing about." Then Sophie would laugh and Julia would laugh too.

Then Julia would respond, "I'm singing about Jesus who loves me so." Sophie would continue to sing her questions and Julia would answer in song. Sophie remembered Julia singing to her and talking about an invisible Jesus. One of the songs Julia sang to Sophie was "A sunbeam."

A sunbeam, a sunbeam,
Jesus wants me for a sunbeam,
A sunbeam, a sunbeam
I'll be a sunbeam for him.

Just like a sunbeam gets its energy from the sun, Sophie came to understand that God was the source of her energy. Many nights when Sophie was older and discouraged with her life, more than anything, she wanted Julia to be right about that sunbeam. She wished she could shine like the sunbeam that received its energy from the Sun. But the pain of that hope was just too much, so as the years passed, Sophie's heart hardened against anything or anyone who talked about a God who cared.

How she wished the tears would flow again from her eyes when she remembered how happy she felt when she sang with Julia at that tender age. When Julia would sing about this Savior, she would tell Sophie how God had felt every pain of his begotten Son.

"Sophia, if you were the only part of God's creation, He would have given the best part of Himself, Jesus, to win you back; that one day, you could be one with Him again." To a seven-year-old girl, this was a wonderful story: that God would love her that much. But all that changed after Julia left.

One cold winter night, while Julia and Sophie had been in the living room, the fire place blazing and the wind whistling outside, they had been so wrapped up in singing one of her stories that neither of them heard Sophie's parents come in. Eyeing Julia angrily, Sophie's mother had stormed into the living room.

"Why is Sophie up so late?!" asked her mother, after she heard them singing about Jesus.

Sophie usually went to bed at 8.p.m. sharp, but Julia and Sophie had been having such a wonderful time singing about this wonderful God, that it seemed as if time had flown by. Sophie had asked Julia to sing more with such excitement on her face that she too was overwhelmed with joy. Julia was so

13

startled at their sudden arrival that she was unable to speak. She knew she was in trouble.

"Why are you telling her fairy tales?!" Sophie's mother asked, glaring at Julia.

Julia was silent with fear, as her eyes bulged out and locked with Sophie's mother. She thought about the consequences for talking about Jesus. Julia had heard all kinds of stories about Christians never being heard of again once they were arrested.

"We want Sophie to grow up in reality, not be immersed in a fantasy world. Don't you know my husband and I could lose our jobs if we believe in this...JESUS?!"

She spat out Jesus as though it were a bad word. While Sophie's mother was speaking with hatred in her voice to Julia, Sophie was trying to get her mother's attention by pulling on her beautiful, glittering- like-diamonds, black evening grown. Sophie was so full of joy, she wanted her parents to know this wonderful Jesus that died for her, so that she might be able to be one with God again.

"Stop pulling on my dress" her mother said, as she pushed her down on the floor. Julia tried to help Sophie up, but then Sophie's mom pushed Julia hard against the wall. "Don't you touch my child; you did enough damage. The child speaks as if she's out of her mind."

Sophie's father picked Sophie up in his arms and said, "Pumpkin, everything is going to be alright."

As she cried, Sophie's father looked at Julia with compassion and gave her a warm smile. He didn't say much though, as he had learned early in the marriage that his wife was dominating and determined to win any argument, right or wrong.

Sophie's mother and father had just come home from a dance that was given to those who were most faithful to the cause of a one world government and religion. Even though the nations could not come to terms to be united as one, they all agreed that religion was one of the main problems that caused war.

14

Meanwhile, Julia was fearful in a religious sense, but felt more fear for Sophie's mother when she said the name of Jesus as if she wanted to spit. All of Julia's fear left her and she felt indignation for God.

Julia braced herself and responded calmly, "It is better to lose your job than your soul."

"Don't correct me! I'm a very educated woman," Sophie's mother said.

She had a Ph.D. in Physics, and she specialized in Astronomy. Her skills included the ability to state and solve problems, to think clearly and logically, and to communicate complex ideas. The government wanted people who could solve everyday problems. Because of the growing population, there was a shortage of clean water; Sophie's mother had to come up with solutions for everyone to get some. Sophie's father had a Ph.D. in Economics, and his specialization was Macroeconomics, so he had to make decisions on supply and demand. Sophie's parents realized the government was looking for scapegoats to solve the over populations issues, and since the Christians defied the new order, they fit the bill.

When Sophie's parents walked in, fear had gripped her mother, as Julia and Sophie sang happily about, an invisible, Jesus. Sophie's mother knew that anyone in her line of work who thought one of her family members was secrecy practicing Christianity, would gladly turn the whole family in to the authorities to grab the high positions she and her husband held. Their lifestyle and privileges would be in jeopardy if the authorities heard that she allowed her daughter to be influenced by Jesus Christ as a reality. Julia understood what Sophie's parents might lose, but knew they were only living for the moment. Julia stood up without saying another word and walked out the door.

The next day, Sophie saw Julia again. With a warm smile, and love and happiness in her heart, she said, "Hi Julia!" Julia looked at her with sadness, and went into her house, without so much as a wave hello. What Sophie didn't know was that her parents had gone over to Julia's house the previous night.

"Julia, if you ever say hello to my daughter again, I will call the police and tell them you're trying to control my daughter's thoughts," Sophie's mother had threatened. Julia had not replied, but the next month she moved away. Sophie questioned her parents and asked why Julia didn't say hello when she spoke to her.

"You see, she's no good," said her mother. But it was hard for Sophie to believe that Julia was no good.

Sophie asked, "Mom, maybe Julia is sick. Why doesn't she come over anymore? Are you sure she doesn't want to visit me?"

Her mother answered angrily, "Don't bother me about Julia! You don't need to be around people who take joy in dashing peoples' hopes! You ask too many questions! Julia said she didn't have time for you!"

"Mommy, maybe we could go and see Julia. I'm afraid she's not well."

"No, she feels ashamed that I scolded her. She wanted to control you. If this Jesus was real, what do you think he would feel about Julia's behavior? So please stop mentioning Julia to me and grow up! This is reality. There is no God, Jesus, or anything you can't see!"

Sophie couldn't fight the spirit of hate in her mother, so she yielded to her will. What Sophie did not know is that when her mother was a child, she had believed that Santa Claus was real. Then, when she was only at a tender age of ten, her parents laughed at her for believing in a fantasy world. Therefore, Sophie's mother had begun to hate anyone that talked about or believed in something intangible.

As a child, Sophie had trusted Julia and believed in her Jesus. She cried until there were no more tears left. She cried because she would never see Julia again or meet this Jesus she was learning to love. Sophie felt as if someone had pulled the rug out from under her. Her parents had drained the happiness she had come to know, and she would never have such hope again. If Julia would have left the day after the incident, Sophie's feelings might have been different, no matter what her mother said. Instead, Julia lived next door to Sophie for a whole month. She lived in one of Sophie's parent houses that they had for their servants for free. Julie could not leave until she found some place else to stay. Meanwhile, Sophie would see Julie every day when she left the house to look for a job and another place to live. Every day Sophie would speak to Julia. But Julia knew that Sophie's mother put cameras outside of Sophie's house and the house she stayed in, and that if she even spoke to Sophie, she would be arrested. So Julia looked at Sophie with a sad look, and a silent prayer that the Lord would take care of Sophie. Julia's heart felt as if it would bust open, but all she could do was walk away.

Sophie grew bitter at the idea of Jesus. She promised herself she would never feel this pain again. After all, Sophie's family had been atheists for generations. They didn't believe in anything that could not be proven. Following in their footsteps, Sophie turned hostile towards Jesus and turned away from hope itself.

After Sophie's world was torn upside down by Julia's silence, she believed her mother when she accused Julia of being indifferent. Ever after, Sophie carried a pain in her heart. To help express these feelings, she started to write in her diary at the age of seven.

"Dear Diary,
Why did you leave me, Julia? What did I do wrong? Mom said you did not want to be bothered with me anymore. She said that Jesus wasn't real."

Sophie did not know what to do with the love she felt for Julia, and the joy she felt about Jesus when Julia sang about Him. Each day she would write something in her diary that expressed her pain. But now, Sophie put the pencil down and started to cry. She cried very quietly. She didn't want her mother to hear her. She didn't want anyone to ridicule her for holding on to the memory of Julia, so she didn't show anyone her diary. As the years passed and she still didn't hear from Julia, the pain became so intense that bitterness started to set in. The only way to relieve the pain was to turn to hate. In her diary, Sophie felt as if she was hitting Julia and her make-believe Jesus, by writing of her with pain and hate.

17

Many years later, by the time Sophie was an adult, she had become a very skilled writer. She wrote short essays to magazines, and published books against Christians, reconstructing their past in a negative way. The church had controlled the European government and the masses before the reformation, and was able to persuade the people to go to war against other religions. She pointed out how the masses were kept in ignorance by officials of the church, who only wanted to exploit them for money and hold them in fear of the afterlife.

Sophie also opened up to the reader about how Christians kept society from advancing forward. Galileo for one was executed by the church for believing that the sun was the center of the universe, and not the earth. Even though the church apologized to the different people that they killed for their thoughts in science, this did not excuse them for the pain they caused so many people. Even now in the present, the Christians expressed superiority over other religions by saying that one only has access to God through Jesus Christ. This thought perpetuated a division from other religious; this is what kept the nations in wars. Slowly, she exposed every weakness in the individuals and groups who called themselves Christians. As the years passed, Sophie became very successful in her writing against their religions. People who did not like Christianity supported her in her work.

Meanwhile, the intensity of the wind's whistling brought Sophie's thoughts back to the present, her hands clenching the steering wheel. The wind howled louder and louder, as if it were a living, breathing entity. It was taunting her, in her mind seeming as if the wind was saying, *What are you going to do now?* Black clouds had gathered in the sky, and It was becoming harder and harder to drive. Sophie felt as if she was moving at a snail's pace. Words could not explain the fear that was gripping her soul.

Her thoughts of Julia made her wonder, *What if the Christians were right? Get a hold of yourself, Sophie! This is no time to get emotional.* Sophie felt as if her heart was in a vise, squeezing tighter and tighter. *What if something happens and I'm seriously injured? Oh God!* She thought jokingly, *if I don't stop saying 'Oh God' next thing I'll be saying 'He answered me.'*

Deep down in her soul Sophie wished there was a God, so she could call upon Him. She dared not though: it was too painful to believe in such a wonderful hope. As Sophie drove, the Lord looked down at her with love and compassion.

"Oh Sophia," He whispered in her ear, "I'm alive and well!"

But Sophie did not let herself hear the Lord. As Sophie was driving, the Lord was filled with such love for the souls of men, while at the same time anger and wrath began to swell up in His soul. He was thinking about Sophie before she was born. The Lord still hoped she would figure out her true assignment on earth.

Chapter 3

God began thinking back to when different thoughts were moving across His mind. In particular, the feeling He felt before He decided to share Himself with Himself, by creating beings that were Him, but conscious of the fact that they could be separate from Him. Had the loneliness been so unbearable that He'd had to bring forth others so unique from Himself? Did He count the cost of rejection? Or did He see the ecstasy of sharing love with individuals who were willing to return His love.

It is said that God took a chance and made creatures with their own individuality with a free will to choose. This decision to make conscious individuals was made by God before the first man was placed on the earth. First, God had to awaken a part of Himself so that they were conscious, individual beings. After He showed them the beginning and the end, He established a council. He gave them the right to vote if they wanted to stay with Him as a whole, or risk being individuals with the right to choose as they wish.

Many decided not to become individuals, but the majority wanted to take the risk. So God asked these conscious beings if they were willing to give their free will back to Him, as there would be a consequence if they didn't give it back. The consequence was this:

"Whatever you decide to do on your own won't be as potent as with me, because it didn't come from the original source."

God began to groan within Himself when He thought back to what it was like when no one was conscious of the fact that He was. So, it is written that God said "let there be," and it was. All that He would be then came fourth. God took a step to lose part of Himself when He gave it to Creation.

God knew that nothing is free. Therefore, a price had to be paid for Him to have complete happiness and joy, to gain love from Himself by His own freewill. So whatever God is, everything that exists came forth from what He wanted to be. Each thought from God/the Source had its purpose. For example, Wisdom came forth from the Source. Wisdom then realized that she was part of the Source, but had her own individuality and free will to choose to be independent of Him. God, who is still all and all, allowed Wisdom to decide how she will run its course.

Every time the Lord projected a thought, an essence of His energy came forth. Those essences came to exist as angels, people, animals, plants, and every other part of His creation. Before the Lord projected these thoughts from Himself, He decided to have a thought full of Wisdom. That thought, then personified, projected its own thought without a connection to the Source. It became Lucifer. Even though he was made perfect, Lucifer was even further from God, but God still gave him the authority to cover the throne, showing he was loved even though he wasn't made with consent.

Wisdom understood what she was, and decided to create her own, just as the original Source did. God did not stop Wisdom because then the very purpose of free will would have been defeated. Even though Wisdom was wise by nature, it could not see that it still needed wisdom from God. Once Wisdom decided to create her own from herself, the connection between Wisdom and God was weakened. Wisdom was weakened because she decided to make a decision on her own. As when you copy a picture, it is never as vivid as the original picture; likewise, when Wisdom took it upon itself to make its own creation, the son of wisdom was not as potent as the original. Yet, God did not reject what Wisdom had created.

The son of Wisdom was identical to his mother, but less powerful and with less responsibility. Yet, God reached out to the son of wisdom and gave him great power and beauty, even assigning him to be the anointed that covered the throne of God. Wisdom herself had free will, but decided not to focus it all on the main source. Her son also had free will, his own individuality, and his own identity; but the son of Wisdom's love for the main Source was weaker than Wisdom's, foreshadowing his inevitable turn away from God.

Instead of loving God with all his heart, Lucifer was inflated by the positions that were given to him. He was the son of the morning, an angel of light, full of wisdom, and perfect in beauty. When he walked, the most beautiful music could be heard. He was covered with every precious stone. He was the angel who covered the Lord's throne with his beautiful wings.

Since God is a spirit, no one had seen Him, unless He took on the form of an angel or man. Nevertheless, all of creation was able to see this beautiful angel Lucifer. All of God's creation that was conscious was given the understanding that one day they would bow to one of the Lord's creation that was a conscious being, who's DNA was only two percent different than the animals. The Lord did not give a reason why every knee would bow to this particular creature. God allowed the angels to see in the future, that this particular creature was called the Son of God. This was not unusual to the angels because many of them were called sons of God, but to bow to one of the Sons of God was confusing. Like Lucifer, many of the angels did not have the understanding that they were god.

Lucifer was distraught. At this moment, sin began to grow in him. He had a proud spirit, and felt that the Lord should have chosen him. *How could the Lord choose someone who's DNA is only two percent different than a beast?* Satan thought to himself, if the Lord of all spirits wanted to pick one of the conscious creatures for angels to bow to, *why not me?* After all, everywhere Satan went in the heavens, earth, and elsewhere, he was admired by most of the angels for his beauty, and wisdom. *I will not bow to a creature so close in nature to a beast.*

"You must trust my judgment. Why do you come against my wishes?" the Lord said to Satan in an angry voice.

"I am part of you. Since I am part of you, I will be independent of you. I will create my own world and bow to no one, everyone will follow me. They will not see you, but they will see me." Satan said to the Lord.

"I will give you space to repent. If you do not repent, I will throw you down as quickly as lighting, and my wrath will come upon you. I need you to give me the glory and pleasure I request," the Lord said with anger.

"I choose not to give you glory and pleasure. I will claim glory and pleasure for myself. I will prove to you that everyone will follow me to seek his or her own pleasure and glory. No one wants you. I was faithful to you, and then you told me that one-day I would bow to one of the sons of God. I will not bow to anyone. Everyone will bow to me. You will see in the end that I will win." Satan said in an arrogant way.

"There is something you forget Lucifer, and that is called love. Creatures of consciousness will choose me, simply because I am God. They will love me because I love them. They will give me glory and honor, regardless of what they receive for themselves. Love is stronger than death," spoke the Lord with compassion.

While the Lord was giving him space to repent, Lucifer had persuaded other angels to follow him. He told the angels that they could be their own gods, creating their own conscious beings, for their own glory. *Just follow me.* Then they would not have to bow to anyone. All the angels could see Satan's beauty on the outside, but some of them could not see his proud spirit. They did not see any judgment come against him when he spoke against the Lord of hosts, so some of them stopped fearing God. Lucifer was able to persuade one-third of the angels in heaven to follow him.

The Lord sent his war angel Michael, and all the other angels to fight against Satan and his legions. The Lord could not kill Satan and the angels because he would be killing Himself. In this way, the Lord prepared a place for them in the center of the earth. It has many names. Some people call it the abyss, the pit, Hades or hell.

Satan never could have imagined that God would take the form of a lowly creature that was just two percent different than a beast. He would be called the Son of God, and He Himself would be the very vessel that would redeem all who needed to be redeemed, including Satan. God needed a body so that blood could be shed. Only God's blood would redeem the creatures of consciousness.

After the fall of Wisdom's son, Wisdom realized her mistake in not submitting her will back to the Source. She thereby repented; but her son did not. Thought his both saddened and angered God, it was all a part of His plan. Therefore, He had in mind a way to win it all back to Himself. By hiding the best part of His nature, He thereby postponed the redemption of his creation until the time was right. This part of His essence would be the one He would use to redeem those which had rebelled against Him, and would be the Beloved Son with whom He would be so well pleased.

■■■

Chapter 4

The further Sophie drove, the more fearful she became. She was driving so slowly now that it almost made her crazy. It had been hours since she'd first gotten into the car, and the desire to stretch her legs was slowly becoming unbearable.

"God help me! Why do I keep calling upon a God that doesn't exist?!" she exclaimed.

Meanwhile, Sophie thought about how she had degraded Christians with the last book she had written, *How Christians Keep Division*. The book argued that Christians were only dreamers, and should thereby be banned from society. She demonstrated that if society were to survive, weaklings and dreamers would have to be pulled out of it, that they would not poison the world's young minds with false hope.

As she continued to drive through the darkness, Sophie was unaware that she was the center of attention in the ongoing spiritual war between God and the Devil. The demons were planning her destruction, and the Lord was allowing it to happen, for the good of humanity.

In the construct of hell, a fallen angel (which most people today call demons) spoke to Satan: "Lord of all evil, why do you want to kill Sophie? She's on our side."

Satan retorted with contempt, "You imbecile, didn't you read her file? She made an agreement with God to be reincarnated and win souls for Christ!"

Another demon spoke, "Lord of the Underworld, if she's on an assignment for the Lord of Hosts, isn't it impossible for us to come against it?"

Satan was furious, shouting, "How dare you doubt my judgment?!" He silenced the demon with a powerful blow. Satan then reminded his demons that he was the rightful god of the world. "After all, I have the power to control the weather," Satan laughed.

A demon whispered to the others, "But only if the Lord gives you permission…"

Originally, Sophie had been born seven hundred years ago. In her first lifetime, she'd kept her faith in God, and when she died, went to heaven. Once she was in the Lord's presence, He asked her if she wanted to be reincarnated for the championing of his glory. He told her that she and a man named Brian were His first choice to fight for Christianity. However, even after she accepted, he did not give her all of the details as to what would happen.

Several angels and God then decided that Sophie's parents would be atheists, because her faith needed to be strengthened for the tribulations ahead. The Lord knew that Sophie would be His enemy. He allowed her to write books against Christians, and even attempt to have laws passed in their opposition. All of this was done for the purification of Christianity. The Lord explained to Brian and Sophie that just as gold is put into the fire to bring out its best parts, so too will Christ's return purify his bride. These are the Christians who have truly given themselves to their faith. Those who were holy will be holy, and those who were just will stay just. Sophie's trials after reincarnation would thus be for her own good. The Lord knew that deep down in her soul, she completely loved Him. In this way, He allowed the forces of darkness to come against Sophie, that he could help her reconstruct her faith in Him again. God wanted Sophie to understand she exists as an extension of His essence, a part of the whole that is God. Soon, she would know the truth.

Back on earth, Sophie looked down at the speedometer; the needle showed ten miles per hour. If there is a hell, I must've died and gone there. She looked out into the darkness. As she cautiously turned around the next curve, she realized she was going uphill.

"Did I make a wrong turn?" She hoped she wasn't going higher up the mountains. The intensity of the situation brought her thoughts went back to her mother. What would she do in a situation like this? She always said, "Think with your head, not with your heart."

While Jesus was watching Sophie driving from the realm of the divine, four angels were discussing her as well.

Two were males, and the other two were females. They all were talking about Sophie.

One male angel said, "I know the Lord doesn't make mistakes, but it seems impossible that Sophia will ever change."

"We all know it's going to work out," said another male angle.

One female angel said, "I know the Lord has chosen Sophia, but even now she won't believe."

Another female angel said, "If only the Lord would bring back her memory before she was reincarnated, so she could remember what she agreed to before she left heaven."

Then the first male angel spoke again, "Then it wouldn't be faith."

The Lord decided to call a meeting. A host of angels came to the meeting. The Lord said, "I will assign many angels to Sophia when Satan sends his demons against her. I will only assign two angles to her now"

In Sophie's mind, she heard a screeching sound, like the scraping of nails on a chalkboard. It was faint; in the distance.

"What is that? She said nervously. "No two vehicles could come together on this road! Besides, I can't pull over! The snow must be two feet high on either side!" The sound grew louder and louder. "Surely, if it's a car, the driver will stop when he sees that he can't get through."

A few hours prior, the skies had been clear, and the evening was beautiful. Moe had only around 10 miles to go before he'd reach the bottom, when he could take a few hours to sleep off his drowsiness. But something inside told him that he should do another quick examination of his rig before he reached the steeper slopes.

"I'll make it," he reassured himself. "After all, there's only ten more miles."

God heard Sophie when she said, "help me," driving up the mountain. Earlier in that same day though, the devil had ordered one of his demons to entice a truck driver that he would not need to check his brakes for his trip.

Sophie saw something big with lights blinking off and on, as if it was trying to speak to her. A screeching sound grew

27

to an ear -splitting crescendo, the lights became brighter and brighter. It was the sound of a horn.

As the driver of the huge semi was trying desperately to give her a message that his brakes were not working, he cried to himself, "Oh God, why didn't I check my brakes?! Please don't let me hurt anyone!" But God wanted the truck driver to learn to be more cautious.

She noticed that the truck was swerving, unable to stay on a straight course. The noise was deafening now, and the light blinded her vision. She watched helplessly as it collided with her vehicle. *Oh God, Oh God!*

Chapter 5

Sophie felt herself floating out of her body and experienced such peace. "What's going on? Where am I?" This was when Sophie realized she was in a hospital, as she stood next to the doctor while he took blood pressure from her unconscious body. When she realized that she was not dead, Sophie braced her spirit arm, expecting to feel it tightening. As the doctor wrapped the device around the arm of the body lying on the bed, having not felt the pressure when she grabbed her arm, she then realized that there is more to the body than what her mother had said.

There she was, there, yet nowhere. She could see her body lying on the bed with a bandage on its head, but she was surprised that there weren't any casts or bandages on her body. It seemed to her that there weren't any bones on her body that were broken, not even a scratch. *This can't be happening.* She knew she wasn't in this world. "Did the God thought get to me? I believed at the last minute. Would I have died if I hadn't called out to God?"

She felt a great sense of loneliness, yet, she still felt at peace. Looking at her body, just by thought, she decided to return to it. She was instantly in her body because of that one thought. However, she could not speak because her body was unconscious; desiring to cry out, though no sound would come. She felt as if she was confined in a prison whenever she returned to her body. It was as if a vise was getting tighter and tighter around her spirit. Eventually, because of the freedom in the spirit world, she decided to leave the presence of her body. Just by thought, Sophie wanted to be on a mountain, and there she was.

Time flowed differently in the Spirit World. It seemed to pass by slower than in the real world. As the months passed by, Sophie began to learn that she could be any place she wanted to be just by thinking about it. She never grew tired, and never got hungry. Sophie even tried to go beyond the solar system, but she could not get past it. So she went everywhere in earth's solar system. Nevertheless, the solar system was her only domain.

She did not feel earthly elements anymore. She had a calm, serene feeling, yet she did not want to be in this lonely state for eternity. She could see people, but they could not see her. It was like living, yet not living. She thought to herself, *this could be hell.*

As the months passed, Sophie went back and forth to her body. One time when she was reminiscing in her body, she heard the nurse say, "It has been five months, and she is still in a coma, and still holding on." Sophie's cousin Walter was present on that particular day. She heard him say, "This is a waste of money if you ask me. Why don't they just pull the plug if they can't bring her back? It would save us a lot of money!" Sophie was horrified, when she heard what Walter said. She knew now that her spirit might be trapped in the spirit world unless she woke up from her coma.

As she was thinking these thoughts, she starts to look at the hospital room. In the room, she was hooked up to a life support machine. The walls were white, and there was one bed and two chairs with a closet by the window. Another nurse walked in and Walter again insisted on pulling the plug, causing Sophie to become further paranoid. *Oh God! Help! What should I do?* Sophie felt afraid because of the way she persecuted Christians and her attitude against God. Sophie didn't know that God wasn't punishing her, but rather helping her to find her purpose. As she was contemplating on what was going on, in walked the truck driver. Walter looked at him with a questioning look.

"I just came to speak with the lady I hit," he said.

"She's unconscious," Walters retorted impatiently.

"I just want a minute."

"Make it quick!" The nurses and Walter walked out of the room.

" I prayed for you, and I believe that God heard me because you're still alive. He showed me that I must be more cautious."

At that very same moment, the two demons that were assigned to Sophie were projecting thoughts to her Cousin Walter's mind. *Her parents didn't even bother to come; they sent you because they believe Sophie might as well be dead since she's only a vegetable. If she died, her parents' inheritance would all go to you. You should insist on pulling the plug so you can get her money.*

While Walter was thinking about these thoughts, his conscience was bothering him because Sophie was like a sister to him. Even though Walter was hard and without feeling with most people, he had a gentle side for Sophie, his first cousin. One particular memory, when he was eight and she was six, he was crying and Sophie asked, "What's the matter?"

"I feel so alone; Mom and Dad are always so busy," Walter had said.

Sophie said, "Someone loves you Walter."

Even though Walter tried to fight his greed for money, the demons' message eventually got to him. He was completely taken over by selfishness.

Meanwhile, God saw the fallen angels trying to convince Walter to terminate Sophie's life. The Lord told Sophia's angels, to go down and convince the doctors to wait before pulling the plug that was keeping Sophie alive.

While the doctors were in a meeting with Walter, one angel spoke in the ears of the ones who were supervising Sophie's care. "Consider the contribution to science if you could revive Sophie."

Shortly thereafter, one of the doctors spoke to Walter directly in the meeting: "I think we should wait another month to do more tests on Sophie before we pull the plug." Many of the doctors in the room nodded at this in agreement.

"I recognize your professional opinion, however I feel I have Sophie's best interest in mind, and I know she wouldn't want to just lay there forever."

Calmly, the doctors reply, "Just give us one month."

Walter says "one month" in an indignation tone, and leaves the room because he is used to getting his way.

During all this interaction with Walter and the doctors, Sophie was standing there in the spirit world listening, *oh God!* Sophie cried in her soul without being heard by anyone. *Lord, wake me up! Don't let Walter pull the plug. I don't want to stay like this forever.* Sophie became desperate and made herself believe in this Jesus. Deep down in her soul, she didn't want to forget when she was seven. In her inner self, Sophie knew that Julia had not forsaken her at an age when her heart was so tender.

The pain she felt in her heart was not a physical pain, but one of knowing that she had hurt the Lord and so many of his people by writing books against Christians. Yet, at the same time, her heart was pounding with a joy she had not felt since she was seven years old. She wanted to cry out to someone that God was alive and well.

Sophie became desperate and started to plead with the Lord.

"Jesus! Jesus! Jesus! The one Julia sang about. I want to know you! I believe! Please forgive me. Help me out of this hell! Send help! Please!"

Chapter 6

As the Lord was looking at Sophie while she was crying out to him, The Lord thought back to before the sons of God shouted for joy. Some will receive my love, and others will have to go through unnecessary suffering without hope until they finally give in to confessing that Jesus Christ is Lord to the Glory of God the Father, bowing to Him, and realizing they were made for My pleasure and glory." This was before any of his thoughts rejected him. The sons of God were the thoughts that had a consciousness. He had several thoughts go thought His mind. I will push out my thoughts and create whatever gives me pleasure, but these thoughts will not be conscious of what they are. Then the Lord said, "How can I receive pleasure in something without consciousness? These thoughts would only be like robots." So He thought again, "I will push more thoughts out, and these thoughts will give me pleasure and glory. They will be conscious that they are separate from me yet part of me." The Lord thought, "I will give them their own free will to choose to love me or not to love me." Then the Lord thought, "what if they choose not to love me?" I will just punish them until they love me. Oh, that would not be love. It would be fear.

The Lord just sat there for a while. He liked the idea of being loved. So he decided to create His thoughts. God delighted in the thought that he would put his very best into humankind. Yet mankind's DNA structure would only be 2 percent different than the very beasts he would create for man. This plan that everything would be Him, yet free to love Him or not as they chose, excited the Lord.

"I will make creatures of every imagination. Some will be powerful and some will be as simple as a child. Those who oppose me will be punished, but I will redeem them with the best part of Myself. I will come in the part of me that is the best one that I am well please with but also the weakest part, which is made flesh, and name Adam. This creature will be made in my image and likeness. He will fail me just as some of the angels will. I will come down and give my heart as a new creation from the family of Adam's flesh. I must have blood so I will give my blood to redeem them back." The Lord started to cry. "Oh, how I want their love. Some day they will be one with Me again. Each of My thoughts is my expression of Myself. Each expression will give me pleasure and glory."

Meanwhile, Sophie left the hospital and went back to her favorite mountain in Yellowstone where she would sit for hours at a time. She settled on the high snowy peak of the mountain because she found it peaceful; it made her feel closer to God. As she was sitting there thinking about her outburst to the lord, the wind seemed to speak as it blew around her. Sophie was surprised because she had not been able to feel the elements in months since the car accident.

She heard singing: the most beautiful sound she had ever heard. The song was "Close to Thee," though she had never heard the song before.

Close to thee, Lord;
Close to thee,
All along my pilgrim journey;
Savior let me walk with thee.

Sophie kept looking all around. She could not see anything.

"Lord, let me see your beauty," Sophie cried.

Suddenly, right before her eyes, all around her there were beings in white robes. Every skin color she had seen on earth was present. There were two angels standing closer to her than the others. In both of their eyes was a look of love. Then she saw someone who was more radiant than the angels. For some reason, she knew that this was the Son of God. Yet, she knew too that He was God.

The Lord spoke, "Hello Sophia, I've waited all these years for your love again."

"Hello Jesus," Sophie smiled. She had not smiled with such warmth and joy since she had smiled at Julia all those years ago.

Sophie looked at the Lord with surprise, and said, "That's the name Julia called me when she was my nanny."

Jesus smiled and said, "That's your name, Sophia. It means wisdom." The Lord explained to her that now that she had returned to him, He wanted her to take on her real name, "Sophia."

Sophia was so overjoyed that the Lord had revealed Himself to her that she could not take her eyes off Him. He did not look like any of the pictures she had seen of Jesus, but she knew it was Him. Sophia felt the same melodious feeling when Julia sang about Jesus.

Jesus had a beautiful tan complexion and hair like soft brown wool. She had never seen beauty like this. It wasn't just His outer beauty, but something inside that made Him shine. His inner beauty was like the peace you feel when it rains after a very hot day.

The Lord spoke again, "Sophia, I've heard your cries. Brian, my servant, will come and work with you. Don't worry; everything will work out for you and Brian."

Sophia thought to herself, *Is this really the Lord?*

Jesus, knowing her thoughts, stretched out His hands. She saw the two holes in his wrists.

"Sophia, don't doubt but believe." Jesus smiled.

She could not believe that this man could love her so much when she had done everything in her power to discredit him.

"I want to show you something that happened before you were born."

"Okay." Sophia said dreamily.

Immediately, the sky lit up. It looked like a movie screen, appearing as if several people were at a table in a ballroom, discussing something important. Sophia was full of excitement as she looked up at the picture. The time was around 1300 AD. Sophia saw The Lord, and another man sitting at a table in a large room that looked like a ball room. She realized that she was born in the same family that she was originally from.

"That looks like me!" her expression was surprised.

"It is you," Jesus said with a whisper and smile.

"Oh! Who's that young man?" Sophia thought he looked handsome; he was tall, with a face that showed compassion. The expression in his eyes moved her because she longed for someone who cared.

"His name is Brian," Jesus replied; "he lived 700 years ago, like you did."

Sophia saw Jesus in the picture, and it made her smile.

"Oh Lord, I do recognize you!" Sophia exclaimed. Jesus laughed.

In the picture the Lord was speaking to Brian and Sophia. He was talking about an important mission he wanted to send them on.

"I will reinforce your faith Sophia. By being starved of hope, you've come to long for it. Once you have been visited by me, and seen that I am real, nothing will ever make you lose that hope again."

Sophia saw herself and Brian, feeling honored that the Lord would send them on this mission. They both agreed to suffer for His name.

"Oh Lord, how I must've have disappointed you. I am so sorry I hurt you."

The Lord hugged Sophia and said, "Be of good cheer, I'm with you always." However the Lord did not tell Sophia and Brian who would be their enemies. The Lord wanted to build up their faith for the task that was before them.

Then, Jesus was gone. Sophia was left on the mountain, alone in the dark. She did not even see a star in the sky. She no longer felt the elements. She felt a great loneliness overcome her.

"I will wait until Brian tells me what do." Sophia said.

While still on the mountain in Yellowstone, Sophia began to look around and watch the morning come. She had never noticed the beauty of her surroundings before. She heard the sound of insects, the singing of the birds. The flowers began to bloom; Sophia noticed the color of the clouds. She marveled at the beauty and wonders of life itself, and how precious they were.

Chapter 7

While Jesus Christ was talking to Sophia, two demons that were assigned to her heard everything Jesus said. The demons then told Satan what God had planned for Brian and Sophia. Much like the Lord, Satan also called a meeting with several of his demons, and two souls that were under his power; Kelsey and Ryan.

Before ever meeting Brian and Sophia, Ryan and Kelsey had been involved with Satanism. While they were at one of these gatherings, Satan called them out to the spirit world above the earth, and brought to their minds the agreement that was made before they were reincarnated to this world. Ryan and Kelsey were somewhat fearful as Satan showed them where they were before. When Satan showed them the reality of them having been in hell in bondage to him, Both Ryan and Kelsey's faces looked as if all life and hope was lost. They never thought of a place of punishment under Satan. They saw themselves in a tormented state. They saw the pain on their faces as if they were hopeless; they knew that they did not have choice when Satan commanded them to make an agreement with him to destroy two people. The only response they could give was, "Yes master, we will do as you say." They said this with false smiles; their inward parts were trembling with terror as they did not want to return to hell, but they did not know how to get out from under Satan's bondage. Secretly, both of them thought, *Why would we want to do evil again when that's what got us into hell in the first place.*

Before Satan had convinced the Lord to reincarnate Ryan and Kelsey from hell, they had lived in Europe during the 1300s. Their hearts were not right with God; they only wanted political power, and the only way to get this power was through the church. Because they were a wealthy couple, the church gladly listened to their advice in exchange for great sums of money. Nevertheless, they had problems with two people who were living in a village in Europe, whose sole occupation was to transcribe the scriptures. While they were there, they had also been telling the villagers of the corruption of the priests that took bribes from the wealthy, that they could control the villagers who were under the church's authority. The two scribes eventually turned out to be Brian and his wife Sophia; and to protect their own interests, Ryan and Kelsey then convinced the church to have Brian and Sophia burned at the stake as heretics.

Since learning of their new mission, Satan noticed that Ryan and Kelsey were hesitant about the implications of following his will again. Satan realized he probably should not have shown them that they were taken out of hell, since now they would recognize the truth of their afterlife. *This was a mistake. I must erase the part of their memories from when they were in hell. I will tell them I want them to rest before their next mission. They will feel they are highly favored by the god of the earth.* So Satan put them to sleep to erase their memory. After that, the only memory Ryan and Kelsey had about this new agreement was that they had been sent against these same two people in the past. Satan reminded them they had done such a good job in the past that he had given them time to rest. Agreeably, they said, "we are here to please you."

After that, the two of them became increasingly more arrogant, thinking they were more important than the others who participated in Satanism. Ryan and Kelsey felt such honor that Satan had chosen them to complete a mission to destroy his enemies, especially when he called them into the spirit world for a meeting. Satan first told them that no matter what they heard about him that was negative, he only wanted to allow them to satisfy the pleasures of the flesh.

"These fools will tell you there is an invisible god that you can't even see," Satan said, "but I am the true God, and I have given you the privilege of seeing me. As my champions though, you must help me fight against my enemies, the most important of which are a man named Brian and a woman named Sophia. They have favor with Yahweh, my nemesis, who they feel is more powerful than I am. But he is nothing in the face of my will."

Back on earth, Brian was a member of a congregation that had just lost their pastor in death. Since this was the beginning of the persecution of Christian churches all over the world, many of the Christians in Brian's church were weak and unstable. Accordingly, Satan tells Ryan and Kelsey they must use charisma, and charm to make the people trust them:

"You must use your wealth to convince the members, and especially Brian, that you are willing to help them with any problems they face, both spiritual and financial. The congregation will be won because they will know your purpose is not just to take from them. You will make the people feel you can make a difference by giving gifts to those in needs. In order to convince this congregation, Ryan, you must marry Kelsey. This particular church would never pick a pastor without a wife. Your job will be to lead and destroy as many souls that you can that belong to that church. Kelsey, I am only going to give you one assignment, and that's Brian. He draws a lot of power from a false god that he thinks is omnipotent. You must make him lose his mind, and thereby his faith."

Chapter 8

Back on the mountain in Yellowstone, a voice suddenly spoke to Sophia: "you don't really believe you saw God, do you?" Startled, Sophia jumped; she had not felt fear since the car accident. She didn't see anyone, but she felt something present. She could tell it was both sinister and evil.

"Lord Jesus, help me," she said anxiously. It was hard to stay on the mountain sitting on this rock. The hardest part was thinking and being tormented in her mind, and not being able to communicate with anyone. This is what hell must be like, trapped, unable to do anything but think.

It seemed as though thirty more days had passed. Sophia prayed to Jesus as often as she could. She had not heard from Him since the day He said He would be with her always. Sophia dared not doubt. Her only hope was that someone named Brian was coming to rescue her. Then, Sophia heard another demon:

"Curse God and you will be put out of your misery."

"No! I won't curse my friend. I will wait for him."

The demon laughed, "You're a fool. Didn't your parents tell you there is nothing?"

Sophia screamed, "You're a liar! My parents were wrong! If there was nothing, what am I doing out of my body? Lord Jesus, Brian, anyone, help me!"

However, while Sophia was being tormented by these demons, Brian was facing his own form of insanity. Overwhelmed in his life, he wanted to commit himself to a mental institution. He was completely torn up inside from the events that had happened with Kelsey. Standing in his kitchen, alone, Brian made a last desperate phone call. He needed someone who had some authority. The assistance pastor and his wife were not close friends of Brian, but Brian had great respect for them.

"Hello, this is Brian, I am bleeding," Brian spoke with sadness in his voice.

The assistance pastor answer with concern, "Are you wounded?" "No, my soul is bleeding, because the love of my life is dead."

Brain told them some of the things that had happened to him, over the years. They both knew Susan, his ex-wife, and they were not surprised when Brian told them some of the things that happened to him with Kelsey in the Spirit World. The Lord knew how much Brian could take, so he sent these two people that would bear him up in prayer. His friends, the pastor and his wife, said this isn't' the first time this incident came to them; others from the mega church have said similar stories that happened with Kelsey and her husband.

Being a mother, the wife knew that if he committed himself to a mental institution, it would be hard to get his children back.

"Think about your daughters," she said.

Brian listened to her. Yet, even though he felt better after speaking to the assistant pastor and his wife, he was still shaken up. His whole body was shivering, and he knew he was on the verge of a nervous breakdown. So, for the sake of his daughters, Brian immediately called a friend to come and watch them for a few weeks. At the very least, he needed to be alone.

Because of his thoughts of the events that happened to him in the past, he felt he needed to hide from himself. The blinds in his room were shut, the curtains, drawn. There was no light in the room; Brain just sat in the dark all day and all night. He shut the sunlight out to hide the bitterness that had darkened his heart. Thinking about the past with his first wife Susan, and the happiness he felt with Kelsey gone, his soul was empty. Usually, Brian would sing and pray and teach his daughters about the Lord, but no sound would come out of his mouth for two weeks. He did not eat anything. He did not even speak to the Lord.

As time rolled on, even though he was still communicating with the assistant pastor and his wife by letters, he feared to hope for happiness. The guilt he had for continuing his actions even after God had told him he was doing wrong turned to bitterness and anger, as he felt God should not have allowed him to be tempted in the spirit world. At that point, Brian knew he was in trouble, but it was just too hard to let Kelsey go. Now that she was out of his life, Brian knew he could not even dare to believe that God would give him hope for happiness again. It seemed like his life would only deal with the spirit world, and all he wanted was a physical reality: a thread of happiness that'd seemed to exist when he'd put Kelsey's love before the love of God. Although he felt pain for himself, he realized he had also caused God to feel pain, simply by choosing something else before Him. He broke out in uncontrollable tears to think that he hurt God the way he had been hurt. However, Brian judged God for the pain that he had been through since he was sixteen, even though he realized that God had had nothing to do with the evil selfishness that mankind brought against each other.

After sitting in his living room for two weeks in the dark, Brian had finally come back to reality; *God is God no matter what I have suffered,* he thought. *Human suffering does not change the fact that He is still God.* At that moment, he felt a warm blanket around him. Brian recognized that it was the spirit of God.

"Brian, repeat this scripture," a voice whispered in his ear. "All things work together for good to those who love the Lord and are called according to his purpose."

But Brian did not respond. He was reluctant to give his all again to God.

The voice spoke again in his head.

"Do what I tell you, Brian."

Brian knew that voice. He knew it was the Lord. Brian said what the voice told him to say.

"Say it again," it commanded.

Brian said it again.

"Say it again." The Lord kept telling Brian to say those words until the phrase was back in his soul. Brian believed the word, but he still could not understand why God allowed him to be abused in such a way. Then, a light appeared out of the darkness, and it formed into a man that looked like Jesus. The expression on His face was that of a love he had never seen before. The bitterness in Brain's heart became stronger from perceiving this perfect happiness and love.

He thought with fear to himself: *is this really God, or am I being delusional?* The instant he had this thought, the light intensified so much that it blinded Brain. In this moment, Brian knew without a doubt that this was God.

"Oh I'm sorry," Brian said with passion, when he realized this truly was God. *How could He love me that much when I did him wrong?*

Brian felt better because he knew God still loved him unconditionally. For the first time in weeks, he felt encouraged by God to get up, wash his face, and eat. While sitting at the kitchen table, Brian thought, *Wow, how much love He has to sit at the table while I have breakfast.* Sitting across the table from Jesus, he started to feel his emotions again. He began to sob to the Lord, apologizing for behaving in such a manner.

"Lord, I'm sorry," he said.

"It's okay, I understand. But I want you to go to someone named Sophia."

"Lord, you want to use me even though it seems as if my faith is gone?"

"Yes, Brian, everything you are going through is for your own good. I know deep down you love me." After Brian ate, The Lord and Brian went into the living room. The Lord said, "I want to show you something." With a wave of His hand, a screen went up like they were going to look at a movie. On the screen, Brian was looking back in time. He saw a big ballroom with chandeliers that looked like crystal candles. There was no one there besides God, Brian and a young woman. The three of them were sitting at a table that sat four people; all four chairs were made of matching maple wood. They were talking and laughing at first, until several angels came into the room. The Lord's face changed from a relaxed expression to a serious look. As Brian was looking at the vision, Jesus Christ brought to his memory the agreement they had made around 700 years ago, for him to be reincarnated back to earth. Still watching the vision, he recalled the choice he and the woman made. Brain remembered God asking if he would come back to earth to encourage the Christians during a certain difficult time period. Brian had agreed, even though he would have to be deprived of love so that he could understand the part of God that longed to be loved.

"Who is that beautiful woman?" Brain said. As he looked at her, it was not only her beauty he saw, but also someone who had the compassion to give herself to humanity.

"That's Sophia," the Lord answered.

Sophia was 5'7," with dark brown eyes and a light tan complexion. Her straight black hair hung half way down her back. Brian was silenced by her beauty.

"I want you to go to her in spirit and teach her how she may give her life to me."

"Yes, Lord."

"No matter what happens, Brian, you must trust me."

Suddenly, Brian was in his room alone. It was a good morning for him. He felt hope. He lay back on the bed and willed his spirit to Sophia.

Chapter 9

Sophia was determined to remain on the tall mountain looking down at the valley. Regardless of her tormenting thoughts of abandonment, she thought: *I must believe; this is my only hope.* Sophia made herself think about something else. She looked around; there wasn't any snow on the mountain at this time. She liked it because it made her feel so peaceful.

Now that she knew God is real, everything about nature became beautiful in a different way. Sitting on a huge rock, her feet in the grass, she noticed ants crawling around her going under the rock. She thought, *I would have never come this far up the mountain before the accident to sit and contemplate on things like ants.* How fearful she was before the accident, and now she was full of hope that made her happy, even though the demons tormented her mind, telling her this was all an illusion. She laughed out loud and thought, *if this is an illusion, I am going to believe that someone is going to meet me like the illusion of God told me.* "One thing I do know," she says out loud, to encourage herself, "I am still alive and that's no illusion. So, I am going to believe what I was told and wait for the promise."

She turned around, and there was a man with a kind expression on his face. Brian had dark brown hair, light brown eyes, and lightly tanned skin. He was around 6'2.

"Hello," he said in a low baritone, with a shy expression.

Sophia did not say anything because she was not sure who he was, although he looked like the man from her vision. No one had ever spoken to her before in the spirit that she was able to see, except for God.

I can see him, yet his body is transparent, she thought.

"Are you unconscious too?' She asked.

"No," he replied. "I leave my body when the master bids me to go on a mission for Him."

"Your master?" Sophia asked, "Who's your master?"

"Jesus Christ," he replied matter-of-factly.

"Do you mean God sent you to me?"

"Yes, God loves you and He is concerned about your well-being."

Sophia started crying hysterically. Brian came and put his arms gently around Sophia and said softly, "It's okay. Everything's okay."

As Sophia sat there, she realized that she was feeling every emotion she had felt when she was in her body. Oh how she loved this man!

Sophia, get a hold of yourself. You can't be in love with him. You just met him!

"Oh, let me introduce myself: my name is Brian, I live in Fergus Falls, Minnesota."

"Hi Brian. I live in the Big Apple; well I should say my body is in the Big Apple."

"What's a big apple? Brian asked.

Sophia laughed, "That's a pet name for New York City."

"Tell me about it," he exclaimed vivaciously.

"Well, what's there to tell? It's big and unfriendly, but also exciting."

"Sophia, would you like to make Jesus Christ Lord of your life?"

"Yes," Sophia answered without hesitation, "I want all of God! Oh, let me know more about this wonderful God. Yes, I will receive and admit I've sinned against a wonderful God. Oh! Jesus, I believe, I believe." Brian looked at Sophia with love and tears in his eyes. He was overjoyed that she had received Jesus Christ as Savior and Lord.

Brian wanted to put his arms around Sophia. *Wow! He said to himself. Why do I feel this way? Is it because she and I are both in the spirit world together? The last time I astral projected was with Kelsey... Or is it the way Sophia looks at me with those beautiful dark brown eyes?*

Brian's thoughts brought him back to when he'd married his first ex-wife, Susan. It was love at first sight. He never wanted to do that again. Even though Sophia was as beautiful as his ex-wife, there was something about the way she looked at him.

As Brian looked at Sophia smiling at him, he longed for her love, a love that he had never felt from Susan. He was looking at her with such love in his eyes that she felt embarrassed, because all of her feelings were showing in her expression. She was smiling from ear to ear. Sophia was surprised that she had sexual feelings for Brian, even though she was unconscious and her spirit was not connected to her body.

Lord, help me, she cried to herself. *This can't be. He is in the spirit as well as I.* Sophia was amazed at all of her emotions.

She thought, *Oh, how much mankind doesn't know on earth.*

Standing there looking at each other, time seemed to slip away.

"Sophia, I believe I'm falling in love with you."

Sophia smiled widely to let him know she was delighted at the idea.

Brian was elated as he spoke to her, "Sophia, I love you so much that I hate to leave you here. It seems as if you are all alone."

"I'm concerned about my family pulling the plug on the machine that is keeping me alive. If you could persuade them that I am very much alive, they might wait until the Lord sees fit to bring me out of this comma."

"I would be more than happy to come and visit you in New York," he grinned. "What hospital do I go to?"

Sophia gave Brian the name and telephone number of one of her relatives, as well as the name of the hospital were her body was. Brian left Sophia in the spirit, and just by thinking, he was back in his body. The first thing Brian did was to make arrangements for someone to watch his daughters. Immediately, he took an airplane to New York City. Brian arrived at the hospital just in time, while several of Sophia's relatives were there, making decisions about when the plug should be pulled.

Brian spoke with determination, "Sophia is alive; you must not pull the plug!"

Sophia's cousin, Walter, yelled indignantly, "She is not alive, she's only a vegetable! And who the hell are you?!" He was convinced that Brian was some kind of a nut case. "You can't come back to see Sophia until you have proven you have a sound mind."

"I'll be back," Brian said, frustrated as he walked out of the room.

After leaving the hospital, Brian looked up a psychiatrist. He prayed that God would give him favor with the doctor. He was blessed, as the doctor was able to see him the same day.

Apart from the evaluation, Brian explained to the doctor his problem. The doctor was also a Christian. He gave Brian a note saying that he had never met a saner person in his life.

Brian went back to the hospital the same night and gave Walter the letter from the psychiatrist. His world turned upside-down, Walter felt afraid. He really did not want to kill Sophia if she was some place alive. Walter told Brian that he would decide in one month as to whether the plug on Sophia's machine would be pulled.

After leaving the hospital, Brian went back to his hotel room. He felt lonely, and he missed his daughters so he decided to go back home.

While waiting for the morning to come, Brian could not sleep in the hotel. Brian felt like he was always in a dilemma. *Why must my life be so complicated?* Brian sat in the dark in his hotel room for an hour; praying for an answer.

Meanwhile, Satan said to his demons that were assigned to Brian, "I want you to work on his mind again. This time make sure he loses his mind completely."

Simultaneously, the Lord assigned Brian two angels, "I want you to encourage Brian as much as possible. Satan is trying to take his mind."

Immediately, one of the angels brought Sophia into Brian's mind. With this memory of her, Brian started to have hope. In fact, he could not get her out of his head. He was thinking about her eyes and the hunger they had for him. That was something he longed to see in his first wife's eyes. As he thought about Sophia, his appetites started to come alive again. The last time Brian had felt this much excitement was when he had been in a trance making love to Kelsey, his pastor's wife at the time.

As Brian sat in his hotel room, he thought about his past. Is this a situation of hoping for happiness just to be let down?

One of Brian angles spoke in Brian's head; *Brian, remember, the Lord said trust him.*

Brian spoke back to his thoughts, "Yes, I know but I'm so tired of the spirit world. Why can't I just meet someone in person? "

The male angel replied, *because you were chosen by God for a special task.*

Shortly thereafter, Brian went to bed.

But the demons who were assigned to Brian were still scheming: *Now is our chance to drive him out of his mind.* They tormented Brian by saying; *God doesn't love you, and look at your life from the time you were born until now. You have been rejected, betrayed, and let down, so how could you trust a God like that?* Brian heard the demons taunting him, but his faith was high because of the recent vision from the Lord. He was not affected by these thoughts anymore, because he knew God loved him.

"Lord, I love you, "he said. "Even if all my life will be a disappointment, I love you for the hope you give us. I trust you Lord for whatever happens with Sophia."

Chapter 10

Brian's father was Jewish and his mother was Palestinian. After Brian's father died when he was born, his mother asked her mother to raise Brian. She felt all torn up inside and was not emotionally strong at the time of Brian's father's death. Brian's father died in one of the many wars in Israel, after Israel had come into their homeland again. Then, when Brian's grandmother died when he was 16 years old, he had to live with his mother and stepfather.

Brian was born in Israel before his mother, Randa, married his stepfather, Ollie, a British Colonel. Randa was going to marry Ollie, but then she met Brian's father, Gilad, who held a high position as a Major. Randa broke off the engagement with Ollie, and married Gilad. Brian's stepfather was emotionally crushed after Brain's father married Brain's mother. After Brian's father was killed, while fighting in the war in Israel, Brian's mother felt it was best if her mother would raise Brian because at the time of Gilad's death, she was emotionally unstable.

While living with his grandmother, Brian was very happy because his grandmother loved him. She made him feel, he was a special gift from God. Brian's grandmother was born in Palestine before Israel became a nation. She was a Palestinian Christian. She taught Brian about Jesus Christ.

Since his stepfather was an Englishman, Brian remembered when he first had to live with his mother and stepfather, and his eight half brothers and sisters in London, England. Every chance Brian's stepfather had, he would find ways to criticize Brian. All of his half brothers and sisters world treat Brian the same way his stepfather treated him in order to find their father's favor. Only Kyle, Brian's year younger half-brother, treated him with love and respect.

In the present, while Brian was waiting in the hotel room in New York City to return home, he woke up sweating with thoughts of Sophia. Brian began to feel sad after he realized no one really loved him. He started to cry. Brian was so staved for love; the only person he felt had truly loved him was his grandmother.

One of the hardest things for Brian to do then was to wait. He dared not even hope for happiness, even though he had seen the Lord in the spirit, and the Lord had showed him what was to come. Brian had suffered so long that it was hard to believe that happiness still existed for him; even though it was easy to tell the Lord he loved Him.

How he wished he could go back and see Sophia in the spirit now. Brian wanted the Lord to tell him when he should leave his body, as he did not want to mess things up now. He must believe that in God's tomorrow, the Lord would come through for him and Sophia. Then, he remembered what happened with his first ex-wife, Susan.

Brian started to cry again as he thought about his first marriage. His most painful experience had been on the night of their honeymoon, when he asked her why she had married him.

"I've suffered so much pain from men in my life; I married you because I want you to hurt the same" she'd replied. "I married you to make you feel such pain that you would never recover from it, just as I haven't. I will always hate you for asking me out on that first date. I couldn't refuse you because the ladies at the church would have known I was lusting after them. Brian, I'm a lesbian, and even now, I have never loved you."

Dumbfounded, for a moment Brian was at a loss for words. The pain and rejection he felt was a harsh blow to the world he had come to know. Susan was so callous with her words; he could not understand why she was being so cruel to him now, even if she did like women the way a man would.

Brian said, "Susan, I still love you, and the Lord can deliver you from your hate."

At this, Susan snapped, and her mind went back to the room she had been kept in day and night. She screamed so loud that Brian could feel her anguish.

"The Lord!?" Susan cursed. "Where was the Lord when I was only ten years old, in a dark room all day without anyone to comfort me!? The only people I saw, if you could call them people, were men who acted like animals. But they used me as if I was even less than that; they used me as their sex toy to satisfy their lust. The only peace I had for two years was when I was allowed to sleep. So don't tell me about your God!" Susan picked up her glass of scotch and emptied it. Taking the bottle, she then topped herself off again as if her life depended on it.

As they were in the midst of this argument, demons looked on to see what Brian would do. Would he still love the Lord?

The angels too were watching; "Oh Lord God, guide Brian to help Susan learn how to forgive," the angels prayed.

"Susan, you must forgive those men. The burden of a lifelong hate is too heavy for you to carry," Brian cried as he spoke.

"Forgive!? Forgive!? Did you say forgive!?" Susan screamed as if she was losing her mind.

"Yes," Brian said softly. Susan snatched the rest of the bottle of scotch and quickly finished its contents.

He remembered with pain her screaming at him, "I don't want you near me ever again! Just looking at your body makes me want to puke."

"I didn't make you marry me," Brian said, his voice starting to quiver. Brian sat on a chair, while Susan lay stretched out on the bed. He asked himself over and over, why anyone would marry someone because of what other people thought. Everything had happened so fast. Susan had said she couldn't have refused him because of what the ladies of the church would think. They would think that it was unnatural to refuse someone as handsome as Brian. Just about every woman in the congregation wanted Brian's attention. Susan didn't know how to deal with her emotions and true nature.

Still sitting in the hotel room, Brian thought back to how beautiful Susan was. The ideal woman of the time, she was 5'7", had blonde hair, a beautiful figure, and a quiet, keep-to-yourself personality. She wasn't the type to chase after men. Even though Susan had initially been cold towards Brain, he thought she had just been trying to act sanctified.

Dating Susan for only two weeks, he had not read the signs of deceit. The tears started to roll down his cheeks as he remembered the first few weeks of their marriage. The first night, Brian recalled how much excitement he had felt. Then, the night of the reception turned into a nightmare. Susan always found someone else to talk to. It seem like she was trying to ignore him.

Brian just wanted to hug and kiss her in front of everyone, but Susan would never look him in the eye. Throughout the entire reception, she found every excuse to stay in the public eye. When some of her friends were leaving, she wanted to hang out with them. She did not want to leave and go to the hotel and begin the first night of their honeymoon. When the party finally ended, he at last convinced her to come with him. On the way, they'd stopped at the liquor store and bought a bottle of scotch; Susan had opened it immediately, drinking and cursing the entire way to the hotel.

When they'd finally arrived at their room, she fought him like a wild cat. When he tried to touch her in any way, she'd spit in his face and comment about how sick his body looked to her. At first, he'd been too surprised to comprehend it her actions, but after hearing her motive, he fell into retreat. Eventually, Brian gave up and just sat in the corner of the room to cry.

Huddled out there in defeat, he'd felt anger when he thought about how Susan had laughed and said, "Do what you have to do and make it quick!" She spoke in such a disgusted tone, Brian wanted to walk out of the room and never look back. But his body would not let him leave. In so many ways, he needed his wife Susan; and she just lay there, sprawled out on the bed.

Brian could hardly stand to see Susan look at him with such disgust in her eyes, so after that night, he'd only had sex with her two more times during the course of their marriage. In each instance, Susan spoke the same cold words as she had on the first night of their marriage. She stayed in the marriage though, because every time she had sex with Brian, she grew pregnant with child. For the same reason, his little girls, Brian stayed in the marriage too.

After ten years of this, Susan could not stand Brian any longer, and ran away with her female lover. After Susan left, Brian was devastated. He was grateful to the Lord though that some good had come out of the marriage, as Susan had left him his three beautiful daughters. Now, his only purpose was those three little girls.

Chapter 11

Alone again in the spirit world, Sophia had not seen Brian for an entire month. To her constant despair, the demons that were there continually tormented her about her past.

"What would your precious Brian think of your three ex-husbands?" One demon asked.

"Oh Lord, I am not worthy of Brian!" Sophia cried. In truth, she didn't even know anything about him. "Lord, Is Brian married?" The Lord was silent. "Speak to me!" She tried to keep the vision of what the Lord had told her in her heart and mind. She remembered God saying that everything would work out for her and Brian.

Another demon cackled in Sophia's ear, "It has been one month since you have seen Brian. What kind of God would leave you here alone, sitting on a mountain, calling his name? All day you do nothing but wait here for them, but they are not coming back. They don't really care about you. They've probably forgotten that you are even here."

Sophia started thinking, even if they came back, while Brian might forgive her for marrying such horrible men as she had, would he forgive her for knowingly persecuting Christians? She thought back to her third marriage. She had been married to him for only two years when the marriage had ended; just as soon as she found out what his sick "occupation" was. Evidently, he would take abandoned babies, and hire people to raise them in homes that no one knew about. Then, when they reached the age of twelve, he would sell the orphans for prostitution. Of course, people—police included – eventually caught wind of what was going on; but because her husband was a powerful man in the community, those in authority had looked the other way. Besides, in light of new world law, children of twelve years and older were being considered as adults. *Oh God!* Sophia started to cry. *What will his punishment be? Would God forgive someone who committed deeds like that?* Even though her parents were atheists, they did not approve of what her husband had been doing. Inevitably, they'd helped Sophia get her third divorce.

The more evil Sophia saw in the world back then, the more she was convinced that there could not be a God. *What kind of God would allow things like this to go on?* Her second husband was not nearly as bad as the third, but he sure was not a saint. He founded an institution that frequently sold cocaine to children, sometimes under the age of twelve. She'd stayed with him for five months.

Sophia's first marriage was her longest though. She stayed with him for five years after her parents had introduced him to her. He was also an atheist, so her parents had been pleased with him right away. But underneath his polite, calm, exterior he was a hateful, cruel villain. He hated everything and everyone, even Sophia. She was a virgin when she had married him. He had treated her with respect and even satisfied her in bed, but he could not stomach humans. He felt they should all just die, and that they polluted the Earth. Many times Sophia would ask him, "What are you? You're human. Why would you hate your own species?"

"Yes, that's why I despise humans; I despise myself. I wake up every day, another day closer to my death," He usually responded.

"Well, do something to help society then. Make it a better place." Sophia would plead, quickly getting tired of his constant depressing mood.

"What for? Man is just going die anyway." Sophia wanted to tell him what she had felt when she was seven, but she dared not though. She did not want to give him any false hope. Finally, she divorced him because she could not deal with someone so miserable. Sophia cried as she sat on the mountain, thinking about her ex-husbands. "Brian is going to think I'm a very unstable person, divorcing three times. Lord please help me." She felt a breeze stir up and heard someone whisper in her ear, *go back to your body.*

Chapter 12

On his way to the airport, something kept tugging at Brian to return to the hospital. Eventually, he turned the car around and rushed to Sophia's room. Walter was there speaking with a doctor as Brian rushed into the room. He heard Walter say impatiently, " I want that plug pulled now!"

Indignantly, Brian yelled, "What!? I thought you said you'd wait a month before you pull the plug!?" Brian then looked at the doctor with prayerful eyes, trying to see if the doctor would have sympathy to stop Walter's determination. Walter's eyes almost seemed to pop out of their sockets with surprise, because he thought by telling Brian that he would wait for a month, Brain would go home. Nevertheless, Walter was determined to pull the plug, regardless of Brian's sudden appearance.   Looking him straight in the eyes with a questioning stare, Brian said with a pleading voice, "just let me call her!?" Glancing at the doctor, Brain's pleaded silently for the doctor to back him up. The doctor then glanced at Walter with a disapproving looked. Walter looked back at the doctor with fear on his face, "I want the plug pulled in five minutes!" Walter was afraid because if Sophia woke up, his whole world would be turned upside down. Walter remembered what Brian had said about Sophia being out of her body.

If Sophia was some place outside of her body, this would mean that there was life after death. If there was life after death, there was a possibility that there was a God. This was too much for Walter to accept. All that he was taught would have been a lie. He felt naked just thinking about it. The only solution was to pull the plug on Sophia's machine. At all costs, Sophia must die so that he could keep his peace of mind. At the same time, if what Brian said was true, then he would be a murderer. Considering the implications of murder, Walter's heart started to melt, as he remembered Sophia's kindness to him over the years. Torn up inside, Walter just walked away from the doctor, allowing Brian to call Sophia.

Meanwhile, Sophia was back in her body. She felt tightness around her as she heard Brian's voice calling her over and over again to wake up. She tried but could not open her eyes. *Oh Jesus,* Sophia screamed within herself. *Please help me to open my eyes!*

Brian continued to call, "Sophia, wake up! Wake up, Sophia!" Brian took Sophia's clammy, limp hand into his own. "Sophia, if you hear me squeeze my hand."

The two demons that were assigned to Sophia had their hands on her eyes. Meanwhile, the two angels that were assigned to Sophia fought with the demons for control. Realizing that they could not fight the angels because of Sophia's newfound faith, they inevitably were forced to retreat, terrorized with fear.

Brian continued to call out to Sophia. Miraculously, he felt a squeeze. Brian screamed, "Look! She's squeezing my hand!" The doctor saw what was happening, and he got so caught up that he started to call her Sophia instead Sophie, as her name was on the chart. He took Sophia's other hand and said, "If you hear me, Sophia, squeeze my hand." Sophia not only squeezed the doctor's hand, but she would not let it go. The doctor beamed, "This woman wants to live. Thank God we did not pull the plug. Walter stood in a corner, silently feeling confused and remorseful, really seeing himself for what he had almost become. Within the next half-hour, Sophia was at last able to open her eyes and speak.

When Sophia first opened her eyes everyone looked blurry, and unclear. Sophia wanted to see Brian. Even though Sophia could not speak clearly, she tried to say something. Brian understood through the spirit world that she was saying, *Brian, is that you?*

Yes, Sophia, I am here. Brian felt as if his heart would burst. He was so happy because now life was a reality. Sophia spoke through her spirit to Brian. *I can't see you clearly, but I like the sound of your voice.* Brian felt so warm inside his soul.

Oh you will see soon enough, He laughed. Sophia laughed with him. Sophia was overjoyed that the Lord had given her another chance to live. Sophia spoke to Brian in her spirit, telling him to thank Walter for taking care of her financial burdens while she was in the coma.

After Brian told Walter what Sophia had said to him in the spirit, Walter simply said, "No problem," and walked away.

Chapter 13

Over the next three months while Sophia was in physical therapy, her eyesight and speech completely returned, and she was able to walk again. Brian talked on his cell phone to Sophia every day about his family and his children's mother. Brian did not want to get too personal about questioning her life, but his interest in her was more than he thought she had for him. In conjunction with his reluctance, Sophia too was afraid to tell Brian what she was before she came to Jesus Christ. She did not want to lose Brian, not because he was 6'2" and very handsome, but because there was something incredibly wholesome about this man. She had never found this quality in other men before. Brian was concerned about God, and people, and had a sad past. When she heard how he stayed with the girls after his ex-wife left, Sophia loved him even more.

"Brian, I would love to meet your daughters after meeting you; I know they must be wonderful." This was when Sophia brought up her marriage. "I never had any children, although I have been married before." Brian sighed with relief and smiled. Sophia felt happy when he smiled because it told her that he was interested in her.

Sophia had been completely restored from the coma, and the following month she and Brian became very close. Sophia grew devoted to Brain for many reasons: he was a friend of Jesus Christ, her savior; he was devoted to his three daughters; she loved the way he looked at her; and the expression on his face made her feel like a queen. Also, Sophia felt a deep love for Brian's daughters. They were so kind and gentle. The two older girls were the exact image and likeness of their father. The youngest daughter did not look like the other two girls, but she still had the gentle qualities of her father.

Whenever Brian and the girls would come and see Sophia, the girls would embrace her. This was new to Sophia because her mother and father had never hugged her or showed her any affection. All of her life she had longed for someone to show her this kind of warmth.

Her mother had taught her to never let any man use her. "Let him honor you in marriage, if he wants you," she had said. Even though her parents were not religious, they had at least taught Sophia moral values.

Once she was released from the hospital, Sophia promised that next time Brian came to visit she would talk about her past. So when Brian came to her apartment in New York City that next weekend, she told him how she had been on her way to sign an agreement that would kill Christians when the car accident had happened.

"Why would you want to kill Christians?" Brian asked in a surprised voice. Sophia explained her family background and what had happened to her when she was seven years old. She felt that such a wonderful story of Jesus should not be told if it was not true. It was worse than stabbing someone with a knife; if you were stabbed with a knife, at least the wound would eventually heal. Her wound never healed. The more she thought about the fact that Jesus Christ was not real, the more she felt the pain of hopelessness, and the more she fought the Christians. Brian was shocked by all of this, but happy that Sophia was being honest with him.

The two of them still did not know about all the secrets of each other's dark past. Brian in particular was worried about the skeletons in his closet. Demons tormented him about his relationship with Kelsey every day.

"Do you think Sophia would believe you if you said you went with the pastor's wife because she forced herself on you?

Brian called out to the Lord, "Lord, how can I tell this part of my life to Sophia?"

"You fool," the demon whispered in his ear, "don't tell here anything about Kelsey."

"Oh Lord, I can't do that. Sophia would know I was hiding something."

Another demon whispered in Brian's ear, "Sophia's going to think you are out of your mind if you tell her Kelsey came through the walls."

"Lord, that's true. Help me Jesus; I don't know what to do."

Brian felt such a peace and heard a voice in his mind say, "Be still." Brian thought about the Bible. I must tell the truth; the Lord will work it out.

Brian had not thought he would ever feel at peace again, but in this moment he did.

Chapter 14

Enticing and flirtatious, Kelsey had a model figure of 5'7", long straight black hair, a creamy Italian complexion, and light green cat eyes. Like a spider, Kelsey wove a web of charm and superficial prestige to lure anyone that she could utilize to satisfy her own desires. She knew how to use her looks to feed into a man's ego. She would create false personas to impress others in whatever situation she was in, demanding their praise. Since she had no parents, she was moved from one relative to another every six months from the time she was born, and she never had a healthy, stable relationship with anyone. This caused her to form a barrier around her hardened emotions. In the end, Kelsey felt so much like nothing that everything else ceased to matter.

She wanted to be recognized by society as something, but couldn't relate to God because she had never known the love of a father, mother, or anyone else to call her own. Kelsey heard about a place where she could receive supernatural powers and do anything she wanted without penalty. Because she didn't have any close contact with God or family members, she did not have any reason to follow morals. So Kelsey's heart became hard as stone. She made up her mind she would get what she wanted no matter who she hurt, even if it meant joining the occult. So when she met Ryan, it was not a difficult decision to marry him for his position and wealth.

Ryan was tall and of a nice build, with striking sky blue eyes, dimples, and a smile that could melted anyone's heart. He had the true Casanova personality. He was born of the elite in Germany, and his family was of the richest two percent of businesses owners in the country. Ryan had everything a child could want, and because of his looks, charm, and status, it came to him easily. He was the oldest of two sisters, and a brother. His father and mother had always treated all of the children fairly, until Ryan began threatening them to give him his siblings' possessions. Only wishing to make him happy, they gave into Ryan's selfish wishes. Eventually, he stopped fearing what his parents thought. At first, Ryan felt powerful, but the lack of discipline caused him to develop insecurity. The more he felt insecure, the more he was hostile towards people. Even though his life seemed perfect on the outside, he was not satisfied, and wanted something to excite and challenge him.

Meanwhile, Ryan's parents were secrets Christians. By age eight, Ryan realized that society believed Christianity was taboo, and he used it against them. But when he got his way, he hated himself inside. Ryan never received Christ while he lived at home with his parents; because to become a Christian, one must humble oneself to God and be as a child. He never learned to submit to his parents or anyone with authority, which cause him to get away with just about anything. Having everything he wanted, he longed for some kind of excitement, even if it was devious behavior.

After Ryan left home for college, he met his new roommate, who for the first time in Ryan's life was dominant over him. Ryan discovered he liked the thrill of it. Everything the roommate demanded of Ryan, he submitted to; because it gave him the feeling of security, of pacification. The roommate, like Ryan, wanted power over people so he could feel like he was something. Due to each other's influence, they joined an occult group that worshipped Satan to obtain supernatural powers. Ryan was not satisfied with just being handsome and rich; he wanted to control people.

Satan certainly had picked the right people to infiltrate the underground churches. Since Ryan was raise in a Christian home, and wanted to control people, he fit perfectly as Satan's first choice. Satan selected Kelsey because she was rejected and willing to do anything to receive praise. The Lord's enemy wanted to make sure that the ones he had chosen for this assignment would not be at risk of falling in love with God, so it was no accident that both Ryan and Kelsey were the results of insufficient parenting. The main assignment for the two of them was to destroy the faith of two people, Brian and Sophia. Satan knew that because of their positions in the world, if he destroyed Brian, it would be easy to destroy Sophia.

The pastor and his wife's purposes were not only to destroy Brian and Sophia, but to destroy the faith of all the members that attended the same church. So far, they had succeeded in deceiving all of the members of the church save a few. The elders of the congregation were the only ones who saw Satan's plans for what they were. The pastor's wife, Kelsey, was supposed to destroy Brian's mind, which had been weakened by his rocky marriage with Susan. Brian's faith was also insecure, and therefore he had a troubled spirit, which affected his relationship with the Lord.

The very idea that he could never marry again filled his heart with tears. Brian wanted so much to be able to love someone that just the thought of it crushed his spirit. Driven by this feeling, Brian never told Pastor Ryan what was going on in his bedroom with Kelsey.

Chapter 15

After getting orders from Satan about their assignment, Ryan and Kelsey had to think of a plan to break up Brian's marriage. Due to a great deal of insight, Ryan eventually told Kelsey his plan to rape Susan, as being raped again would likely put her over the edge. Kelsey knew Brian would become bitter with God if his wife left him. Once Susan was gone, Kelsey knew she had a chance of winning Brian. Ryan lusted for Susan's beautiful body, and Kelsey lusted for Brian's sexy one.

Susan's daughters were at Brian's step-brother's house for an overnight stay, while Brian was at work. On her own at home, she had time to think about her marriage that day, and how she was treating Brian. She had been thinking that he was really trying to understand her lately, so she began to consider how she might change the way she usually felt when she saw his body. It seemed sort of ridiculous in her head, but the thought of what it could mean for her and her children made her smile. While Susan was dwelling on all this, she saw something coming through the walls like a shadow; and then the more she looked at it, the more it began to take on the form of a man. To her horror, as she looked, she realized it was her pastor.

"Pastor Ryan?!" she exclaimed, "What's going on? How are you in my house?"

"Fret not child, all will be revealed in time" he promised. "You're going to love the message I've brought for you..."

At first she didn't understand, but as Ryan began to approach her, she recognized an all too familiar hunger in his eyes. As the memories and the situation threatened to overwhelm her, she grew frozen with fear. His sickening grin testified to her every suspicion. In her final moments of clarity, she watched as the pastor forced himself upon her, enveloping her world with pain and shadow.

After it was over, she dared not tell anyone about what had happened; she knew that no one would believe her. Susan was inexplicably tormented every time Brian asked her to attend a church service. She did not know how to tell Brian or anyone of her rape. Eventually, during a random visit, Susan broke down to her foster mother about how she could not stand to be touched. Her foster mother thought she understood completely; as she was the one who had rescued Susan from the dozen men who violated her day and night when she was only a child. Susan wanted to tell her foster mother what Pastor Ryan had done, but was afraid because she did not want to sound crazy. Her foster mother told her that maybe it would be best for her to leave Brian; after all, he was innocent of the evil that was done to her in the past.

"What about the girls!" Susan shouted with tears running down her cheeks.

"I know it will hurt you to give Brian their custody, but I think Brian is a good father, and you need time to yourself to work things out. Besides, I think it would be unfair for you to try and teach the girls to respect men."

Susan's foster mother looked at Susan with pain in her eyes, but couldn't back down from what she knew to be true. Afterwards, Susan had planned on taking her foster mother's advice, but less than a month later she realized she was pregnant. Susan knew it was not Brian's child, because she had only let Brian have sex with her once since their honeymoon... And each time she had sex with Brian she had become pregnant. In this way, Susan found herself in the dilemma of a lifetime. She dared not tell anyone about what had happened to her at the hands of Pastor Ryan. So Susan allowed Brian to have sex with her again, and allowed him to be overjoyed when she told him she was pregnant again.

When the baby was only two, Susan quit going to church altogether. She couldn't stand being there with her husband when she knew that her last baby was Pastor Ryan's. Meanwhile, Brian did everything in his power to try and make Susan happy. He did not approach her sexually anymore because he had seen how it caused her so much pain emotionally. However, he could not understand why Susan insisted upon giving up going to church. Even stranger, on the holidays when she could be convinced to join the rest of the family in service, she would get incredibly pale for the duration of heaping the pastor's sermons. Brian admitted to himself that they could be a little too "fire and brimstone" at times, but that had always been the nature of Ryan's services. Besides, he never made hell sound that scary.

Chapter 16

As time went on, Susan found that she could stand Brian less and less. Needing someone to talk to, her foster mother introduced her to a woman with whom she felt very comfortable. At the same time, she felt guilty because Brian had never given her a reason to be unfaithful. In fact, she knew that Brian had tried everything within his power to make her feel comfortable with him. Susan had trouble with her coldness towards her husband; she wanted to be kind and loving towards him, but she just couldn't get over her torment at the hands of men. She didn't have a good image of her father, and had never had role model of a decent man before Brian. To make matters worse, she did not know how to explain the incident of Pastor Ryan walking through walls and sexually abusing her.

Susan found herself on a fence, and she knew she could fall either way with only a push. With all the courage she could muster, she decided to confide in the pastor's wife, Kelsey.

When Susan told Kelsey everything she had been through, especially her falling for a particular woman, she felt more relieved than she had in a long time. However, Susan did not mention to Kelsey about Pastor Ryan walking through the walls and assaulting her sexually. Kelsey told her she should leave Brian and just stay single, because it wasn't fair to Brian to be neglected. Susan was a little disappointed, because she wanted to stay with Brian for their daughters. She was hoping that they could pray for the pain and hurt she was carrying to be healed, that she would at last be able to trust and love Brian for the good man he was.

So Susan took Kelsey's advice when she was told that her nature would always be the way it was. Though regrettably, Susan decided she would now take the advice of her foster mother as well. It was time to leave Brian.

Brian could not understand why the Lord was allowing him to go from one turmoil after another. He was trying to raise his three little girls, and trying to explain to his daughters why their mother had left. Brian did not know how to get in touch with Susan. She only left a note saying that she could not take anymore. Brian had to deal with his oldest daughter, Laquasha, emotions, because she missed her mother the most. It was worst for Laquasha because she was nine when her mother left. *show* Laquasha would cry a lot. Brian remembered the teacher calling from Laquasha's school and saying that she cried about everything. The teacher became concern because Brian told her that LSaquasha's mother had left. Brian would take Laquasha in his arms and say, "pray for mommy. She needs to be alone right now." Laquasha would pray, "Dear Jesus, please protect my Mom. Let her call us. I miss my mom."

Brian's second daughter Nadia was four year old when Susan left. She did not say very much. For three days straight she asked, "Daddy, when is Mommy coming home?" Brian' heart was broken; he did not know what to say. On the third day, Brian picked Nadia up and said, "Let's pretend Mommy went with Jesus." Nadia smiled and said, "Okay, daddy." Nadia never asked about her mother again. Brian's youngest daughter Diane was only two years old when Susan left. Diane showed emotion in a different way than her two sisters, she did not understand the concept that her mother wasn't coming back. She would come into Brian's room in the morning and say, "Mommy?" She did this for four days in a row. Brian would take Diane in his arms and say, "Mommy is not here right now, baby."

After a month the youngest daughter forgot her mother. The second daughter forgot her mother after four years. The oldest daughter never forgot her mother. Up to the present time, this was the girls first Christmas without their mother. It was a sad Christmas but Brian tried to make up the sadness with the gifts he brought the girls. It was December 31. Brian was so overwhelmed with everything going on in his life. Brian thanked God for his goodness. He found one of the older mothers in the church to watch Nadia and Diane, while Laquasha went to school. The Lord had blessed him to keep his job at the high school as a biology teacher. Brian was able to be home with the girls by 4 p.m.

After his wife Susan had left, the pastor's wife Kelsey had found her way in the spirit world into his bedroom. Therefore, New Year's Eve was so emotional for Brian. Here he was making love to Kelsey in the spirit world and could not even tell his daughters how much he love this woman. Brian did not know that Kelsey was divorced from Pastor Ryan, and that they did not even live in the same residence. Nor did Ryan's members know.

Brian remembered being so overwhelmed. He had just confessed to the church that he had committed adultery. His first wife Susan had left him three months before he confessed to the church. Brian confessed because he loved praising the Lord. The demons tormented him. They said, "You have no right to praise god any more since you sinned with Kelsey!" Because Brian treasured praising God, he was willing to humble himself before the church. He was hoping that someone would pray for him. Instead of someone coming up to him and saying, "Brother Brian, I will pray that the Lord will give you grace to resist temptation," the only people that came up to him were people that criticized him for confessing before the church.

Brian Continue to remember how he sat on the floor in the living room, the curtains and the shades were closed. It was very dark in the living room. Brian's daughters were asleep, and they were used to Brian crying and praying to the Lord. He loved it when Kelsey visited him but he felt that she was only thinking about relieving herself. Brian wanted to be loved, not use. At this point in his relationship with Kelsey, he did not know how he felt after he confessed to the church that he had committed adultery. Brian did not want to think any more about right and wrong. All he knew was that Kelsey brought happiness into his life. He also had happiness by being a father, but he wanted a wife that loved him and his daughters. Madly in love with Kelsey, lack of support from the church, he gave in to seeing Kelsey, justifying that it was not wrong.

As Brian sat there on the floor, he felt as if he was doomed to a life of continual abuse. He cried for three hours. Between the hours of midnight and 6 a.m., there was a great light in front of him. Brian looked up and there was Jesus Christ looking at him. At least he looked like the pictures he had seen of Jesus hanging on the wall. Brian was hurt with the Lord. Brian was saying in his subconscious, why did you let me be in this situation? I just wanted to please you.

The Lord was smiling at Brian with such love in his eyes. It had seemed to Brian that the Lord was saying to him, I am pleased that you confessed that you have sinned. The Lord did not condemn Brian for being in the situation with Kelsey. Brian went into a peaceful sleep after the Lord vanished. It seemed to Brian that the Lord looked at him for a minute. This event happen before Brian was able to leave his body and go to heaven.

Chapter 17

Every chance Kelsey got she would show immense kindness to Brian. He would come home Sundays thinking about Kelsey, as he slowly fell in love with her. The reason Brian had her on his mind day and night was because Kelsey would leave her body and talk to Brian's mind. She would say to him over and over, "You know you want Kelsey; see how she looks at you." Kelsey would project these thoughts to him four times a day, though Brian could not understand why Kelsey was on his mind.

What Brian did not understand was that Kelsey was using witchcraft on him by projecting thoughts to his mind. Whenever a person uses hypnosis and suggests things to another, it causes that person's personality to be subject to the other person's will.

Brian tried to think about the Lord. He tried to show affection to his wife Susan, but all she did was make him feel like dirt. Brian tried not to lust after Kelsey, but he could not deny his attraction to her. Often, he could not wait to go to church. He just wanted to see Kelsey. Brain was satisfied with just a smile from her. One day, Brian could not stand it anymore. His want for Kelsey burned like a fire that threatened to consume him. "Lord, please help me!" he cried.

Whether the next move he made would be to entice Kelsey to leave him alone, or to leave her husband, not even Brian knew. Before he gave the Lord a chance to respond, he decided to write Kelsey an enticing letter. Brian wrote a steamy, sexual letter filled with his love for her. He was hoping to provoke her and make her angry with him. Rather, Brian's subconscious mind   either wanted Kelsey to say something to him, or just to make Kelsey angry; that her love for the Lord would rebuke him and hopefully ignore him. At the end of the letter, Brian told Kelsey to burn it because he did not want Ryan to find it. Brian did not want to break up anyone's marriage, but he wanted Kelsey to stop being so affectionate to him, especially with her hands. The willingness of her touch on his hands was more than he had ever received from a woman before. The turn on was more than he could stand.

The only one who Brian told about this was his formerly bisexual half-brother, who was now married with six children: three daughters from three different women when he had been a practicing bisexual and three sons from his current wife. Brian's half-brother Kyle was kind as well as handsome. Kyle had come to Jesus Christ, and the Lord had changed his life. Brian felt very comfortable talking to Kyle about his feelings for Kelsey.

Brian loved Kelsey; no woman had ever made him feel so turned on. Not only by touching his hands, but also by the way she stared right into his very soul. He could see in her eyes that she wanted him. Brian needed to believe that it was love coming from the pastor's wife.

The worst mistake he made was when he told Kelsey how he felt about her. After that, she showed even more affection towards him. One night when the children were away at a close friend's house, Brian was lying in his bed thinking about Kelsey. He was not sure if he was dreaming or in some kind of trance. He could see everything in his bedroom but he could not move, it was like he was paralyzed.

And there she was; Kelsey stood by the bed as naked as the day she was born. She put his hand on her vagina. Brian tried to pull away but his body would not move. There was no hope for him to not be sexually aroused. Having gotten what she wanted, Kelsey climbed on top and raped him. Brian was sure that was what happened. Kelsey did not say anything; she just took the liberty of pleasuring herself on him. Then, she walked through the walls and left. Brian was distraught.

"How could Kelsey have done that?" he inquired to himself. "She was here, and then she went through the walls." Brian was puzzled. "Lord, have mercy. I know it was Kelsey on my body having sex with me. I know it wasn't just a wet dream. I saw her disappear through the wall! Oh Lord, how did she get in my house? The doors are still locked!" Brian didn't know what to do because he felt that he had no one; Susan had just abandoned him, and he wasn't sure of whom to go to. "Now Kelsey is coming to me as a spirit?" Brian was not sure if he had dreamed it, or if it had actually happened in the flesh. He had felt everything; but he would never have had sex with Kelsey on his own.

Brian had come to God when he was a young child. He'd been only nine years old. His grandmother had been the one who had taught him everything about Jesus. Ever since then, he'd never wanted to hurt the Lord. He tried hard to remain a virgin until marriage, but when he made that commitment, he had wound up with someone who was clearly disgusted with him.

Brian felt a sharp pain in his heart against the Lord, because he'd wanted to do the right thing. He thought, *how can you do the right thing if your own wife does not even want you? And now the pastor's wife is forcing herself on me?* The worst part was, he could not explain what had happened to anyone.

Brian started to cry.

Chapter 18

The Lord spoke to his angels: "As long as Brian is in love with Kelsey, he will be under her power, so Brian must surrender his whole being to me. He must understand true love is to be given back to the creator first, and then he will be able to love the way I want him to love. Brian can then understand that true love would not only seek to satisfy his lust, but the whole of the self. When Brian gives himself totally to Me, he will be able to give himself totally to someone else. He must see that Kelsey is only concerned about satisfying herself. Kelsey does not know how to love Me or anyone else. She doesn't even know how to love herself. To love the self is to give all of ones being for the rescue of someone else. So both Brian and Kelsey must cast all their cares upon me."

Satan spoke to the two demons assigned to Brian: "Make him curse God; I could use someone like Brian on my side."

One of the demons replied, "He is hidden in Christ. We cannot reach his spirit!"

"Never mind all that!" Satan demanded, his flesh can still be turned over to me if I can get a hold of his soul. Until then, work on his mind, his will, and his emotions."

Immediately, one demon spoke to Brian's mind. "Why do you hold on to your belief in God? Whenever you put your trust in Him, the only thing that comes your way is more sorrow?"   Nearly defeated, Brian replied to these thoughts, "Because I love Him."

"Why do you love Him?" The demon questioned again.

Brian said with finality, "Because He is what hope is." At this, the demons left Brian, as they themselves began to wonder why they did not love the Lord.

Chapter 19

The pastor and his wife were good at transporting their bodies anywhere. All they had to do was think of a place, and they were there. *Who's going to believe Brian anyway? He dares not tell anybody*, thought Kelsey. With all of her talents, rarely was she to worry more than this.

Brian meanwhile already felt uncertain in his connection with the Lord because of his marriage to Susan, and after his encounter with Kelsey he was continuously dismayed. Brian loved the Lord. He always sang praises to Him no matter what happened in his life. In church, he sang with all his soul. He taught his daughters about the Lord and even had praise services held in his home. All this he continued now, as a tribute against the lustful evils in the world.

Yet even so, Brian was happy when he saw Kelsey in church, because he felt such love coming from her. Brian began to wonder though, *was it love or lust*? He continued to ask himself over and over how Kelsey could do this to him. But he should have asked the Lord.

"How did she do this to me?!" Brian cried out. "She knows I cannot tell anyone that she came into my house without opening any doors." In his heart, Brian would not have had sex with Kelsey if he had not been forced. In fact, he probably would have persuaded her to marry him instead. All of this made him furious! He felt a double pain. First, Susan had rejected him as if he were some kind of masculine filth, and then the pastor's wife, whom he thought loved him, used him as a "piece of ass."

The worst part was, Brian could not even tell anyone about these feelings except his half–brother; and when he told Kyle about what happened with Kelsey, even he did not believe Brian when he said that she had come to him when the doors were still locked.

Kyle had simply said, "Oh, it was surely a demon."

Chapter 20

Sophia was a free woman in love. She was going to have her first date with Brian. At the thought of it, her heart raced. She kept asking God, "Is it all for me? Lord, he's so handsome. He has such a beautiful heart, and he has been hurt." Sophia was still moved from when Brian had told her about his daughters, and how he had been taking care of them for the past five years, after his ex-wife Susan had left him.

Meanwhile, Brian's heart was racing at a similar speed as Susan's. "Oh God, help me. Is this really happening? Someone is really in love with me. I am so afraid to tell Sophia about Kelsey; she believes I'm this great person and I'm not. Lord, what shall I do?"

As Brain was getting dressed in his navy blue suit, light blue shirt, and navy blue tie, he heard voices singing audibly, "Peace, peace wonderful peace." Brian had heard male angles sing before, but he had never heard a melody like this.

Brian called his girls, "Girls, do you hear this music?"

"Yes Dad, is that the radio?" they inquired innocently.

Brian laughed and said, "That's no radio."

Then the girls came running to the room their dad was in, asking with smiles, "Well dad, then where is the music coming from?"

"The Lord has sent his angels to cheer me up." he said, motioning for them to come to him. They ran into his arms, and Brian started to laugh with tears of joy because of God's love for him. "It is an answer to my prayers; the Lord is telling me to have peace. He wants me to tell Sophia about Kelsey."

"Will she be angry, Dad?"

"No, the Lord says it's going to be peaceful."

Brian drove over to the park and arrived about an hour early. It was a beautiful day. It was warm, and the wind was blowing as a soft breeze. The pigeons were eating crumbs that were being tossed to them by the children in the park. Brian sat on a bench under a beautiful willow tree; the smell of the air was so fresh. A man was selling hotdogs nearby and the smell came to Brian's nostrils. Brian was smiling because he did not know when he had last been so happy. Yet he was afraid that it couldn't really be happening to him. He had reached a peace in God about talking to Sophia about Kelsey. Brain was still sitting on the bench in the park. Only fifteen minutes had passed, but it seemed like an eternity. "Lord, I'm so nervous, help me." Sophia lived only two blocks from the park.

Sophia was also looking at the clock at that moment. "Lord, only 45 minutes to go. I hope I look okay. But what do I say to a holy man? Oh Lord, I'm so nervous. It feels like I have butterflies in my belly. Please help me to calm down." Almost immediately then, Sophia felt a calm spirit come over her as she looked in the mirror at her white and sky blue dress. Sophia smiled as she remembered the precious night, talking to Brian on the phone about what they would wear on their first date. They both had agreed to the color blue.

Brian though back as he looked at his watch, he remembered back during a time when he was in a hotel, and did not even know how he had gotten there. Kelsey was on top of him making love. Brian remembered what he felt when he'd said, "what are you doing in my bed" He felt angry yet excited. He felt sad because he wanted to push her off him, because he did not want to hurt the Lord anymore. Yet, he did not push Kelsey off him.

He heard Kelsey saying in a sexy tone, "this is not your bed."

His voice got weak then, and as she started to kiss his cheek, he said almost in a whisper, "How did I get here?"

He remembered how Kelsey had then looked into his eyes with her green ones, seemingly reaching into his very soul: "I called you on the phone and you came to me."

"Stop lying in the name of Jesus!" He knew he could not fight her without the Lord's help. "Kelsey, you can't come against my will." Brian jumped up, put on his clothes, and ran out of the hotel. The hotel was only an hour away from his house. While driving home he kept saying to the Lord, "I'm so sorry. Lord, I can't hide it from you. You know my body is all excited. Please help me!"

Later, as Brian sat on his sofa waiting for his girls to arrive home from school, he was incredibly overwhelmed. "Oh God! I'm at your mercy. I can't fight my body or Kelsey's spirit. Lord, how do I fight Kelsey when she puts me in a trance over the phone? I am under her wishes to do with as she pleases. Lord have mercy." Brian remembered also crying out to the Lord, "I am trying to live right! Lord, how do you fight something that you're not so sure you're fighting?!"

As Brian was crying out to the Lord someone touched his shoulder. Brian looked around, and there was Jesus Christ looking back at him with the most undeniable love in his eyes. Brian said, "Lord I'm not worthy for you to come to me." But the Lord rebuked Brian, "I died that you might be worthy to be in my presence!" It seemed to Brian that the Lord showed Himself for five minutes before he vanished.

Brian had thought about what it was like to be in the presence of God. He wanted to cry because he really did not want to keep hurting Him, yet he knew he had to put God before his own flesh. He was crying out to see her; yet, his spirit was hurting to please God. It seemed as if Kelsey was on his mind all the time. He even tried to do things to keep her off his mind. What Brian did not know was that Kelsey was projecting thoughts to him to make that impossible. *Brain you know you miss Kelsey.*

After two weeks had passed since the night with Kelsey in the hotel, Brian continued to think of what had happened to him with Kelsey. One night he found himself in a trance. He was first able to resist Kelsey. "No, "Brian said in a firm voice. He refused to look in Kelley's eyes. "Unless you marry me I can't keep hurting the Lord. I'm tired of this. You have to marry me in the natural way, where everyone would know we're married. I want a marriage certificate."

"Brian, I told you I couldn't. Many souls might even leave Jesus if they found out that we're married."

"Like you care about souls," Brian said sarcastically.

"Brian, don't you care about souls?" Brian did not respond. "How much more so if I marry you before the whole church, after I told the congregation they couldn't marry twice. So many of them left happy second marriages because they trusted my ex-husband and me, that it was God's will. Sweet baby, let's just enjoy ourselves."

"I want to see you, not just in my bed. I want you to be a mother to my girls," Brian said. He sat up and ran his hand through his hair. Kelsey leaned over to him. The smell of her perfume was intoxicating; the touch of her soft hands melted him. It was all too much.

Chapter 21

Brian looked at his watch. He had ten minutes to walk over to Sophia's apartment. Even though he was now thinking about Kelsey, he knew he had to get her off his mind. Otherwise, he would not be able to give his whole heart and honesty to Sophia. Brian talked to the Lord, and said, "help me get Kelsey off my mind." Yet he did not want to forget Kelsey.

He did not know how to handle this new happiness with Sophia, as it was a reality, and Brian realized he had grown to accept some things that weren't. His feelings for Kelsey were something he understood even thought they weren't a part of a healthy relationship. Thinking about Sophia made his heart beat so fast he thought it would burst out though, as it was hard to believe that he was now in a real relationship with someone he loved. Brian heard the Lord Say, "Calm down Brian. What's for you will be for you." At that blissful idea, Brian just laughed. The air was cool, yet nice enough for two robins to sing up in the willow tree. The cool breeze kept the insects from annoying him.

Meanwhile, Sophia looked at the clock anxiously. "Oh Lord, Brian will be here in ten minutes. What should I say?" Sophia felt the Lord's grace. Brian was thinking about what he should say also. Should I give her a kiss?

Brian rang the doorbell; Sophia opened the door. He smiled and said, "Hello, pretty flower."

She laughed. "Well hello sweet dove."

He grabbed her in his arms and hugged her tightly.

Sophia laughed again. "Well come on in." Sophia and Brian's hearts were both beating fast. They said, simultaneously, "My heart's going to burst." They both laughed. Sophia walked over to her stereo system and turned on a Sam Cook CD that she had recently bought. "Dinner will be ready in a few minutes," She said, walking over to the kitchen.

"Do you need any help?" Brian called from the living room.

"No," Sophia called back, surprised that he'd offered to help.

"Would you like some anyway?" he inquired playfully.

"I suppose you could pour us some wine," she ceded with a blush.

After they ate dinner, they danced to the romantic music. "It's 8 o'clock; maybe I should go," Brian said.

Sophia smiled, "The night is young." They held hands while sitting on the sofa.

Turning his body to face her, Brian said, "I want to look in your eyes when I talk to you."

Sophia smiled, and said the only word she could then come up with: "Okay."

"Sophia, I didn't tell you everything about myself."

"Brian, I didn't mention everything to you either."

"Before we get married I want everything laid on the table," Brian said.

Sophia smiled in disbelief, "Brian, did you just propose to me?"

Brain laughed, "Oh Sophia, I'm sorry...Will you...marry me?"

"Brian, let's put everything on the table, as you put it, and see if we even like each other afterward. But I believe my answer will still be 'yes' Brian."

Brian looked at Sophia with a serious expression on his face, "Likewise, I can't imagine ever not having you in my life again. May I turn off the music?"

"Yes you may," Sophia said. Brain got up and disappeared into the living room. The music was turned off and the only sound in the house was the hum of the refrigerator. "Do you want to talk about yourself first?" Brian asked, when he came back from the living room.

"No, I'd rather you go first," Sophia smiled

"Sophia, I already told you about my first wife, Susan."

Sophia laughed, "Brian what do you mean by your first wife?" Brian had a troubled look on his face as if he was going to cry. Sophia grabbed his hands. "Relax, Brian."

"What I'm about to tell you might sound insane. After Susan left me, I became involved with the pastor's wife." Brian paused briefly. "It took place in the supernatural world, though sometimes I wasn't sure if it was only there. Many times I found myself in the same kind of trance. Sometimes, I would find myself awake in a strange hotel when I didn't know how I had gotten there."

Sophia just looked at Brian with wide eyes. Before her car accident she would have thought, this guy is crazy. Nice job Sophia, you meet a decent guy and he is loco. Yet, in her heart she believed him. After meeting Jesus in the vision, and seeing Brian in the spirit world, she had started to believe in the supernatural. Her heart began beating faster. What Brian was saying was for some reason exciting her body. "Brian, I believe you."

"Sophia, I'm not finished."

"You made love to someone in the supernatural," Sophia said in a quiet voice.

Yes, her name was Kelsey; I married her in the spirit before she broke my heart." Brian said.

"Broke your heart, what do you mean?" Sophia asked.

"Right after I married Kelsey in the spirit, there was an event in my old church. Kelsey's ex-husband was sick. So the church came together for a retreat to pray for the pastor. My half-brother, Kyle, told me about it. I wasn't going to the church at the time, nor did I live in the same city as Kelsey anymore. We'd only met in the spirit. I couldn't stand it anymore, so I called her and told her I was coming to the retreat. She didn't really say much on the phone, but when I arrived at the retreat, Kelsey treated me as if I were the scum of the earth. All of the pain I'd felt from my first wife came back to the surface then. All the pain that I'd felt from my stepfather also overwhelmed me. Kelsey was acting as if she didn't even know me. So I left the retreat with my three daughters and a broken heart. I felt like a fool. What was I doing with my life?

I was making love to this woman anytime she felt like it. Yet, I couldn't even go to a retreat and get a warm smile from her."

Sophia started to cry. "Why were you afraid to tell me?" Sophia asked.

"Because you thought I was so holy," Brian said.

"I still think you're wonderful, Brian. What happened after you left the retreat? You said that Kelsey was your wife," Sophia asked.

"Kelsey had the audacity to come to me in the spirit a few nights later, as if nothing had happened. She didn't even apologize. I felt as if I was only a piece of property to her, so I told her that if she ever came to me again, I would blow her brains out," Brian said with a repenting heart.

"Did she come back again?"

"Yes, she cried to me on the phone and said she couldn't stand not seeing me. She wanted me to marry her. When she called me though, she herself was dying. But I loved her so much that I married her. We were married for three weeks before she died. I know this part is hard to believe, Sophia, but the three weeks we were married and I could be with her in the public, I never once made love to her. She had a rare disease, and she was far too sick for anything of the kind. The doctors could not even help her. So, every night I held her in my arms until she fell asleep. She eventually got right with the Lord before she died. I didn't want to go on though after she passed. I wanted to commit myself to a mental institution because I had loved Kelsey that much. About a month after she died however, the Lord had some saints persuade me not to commit myself to a mental institution. They told me to think about my daughters. Still, I cried myself to sleep every night after Kelsey died.

One night the Lord eventually appeared to me. He told me about you, and before we ever even met, the Lord showed me a vision of our future." Sophia was still holding Brian's hands.

"Brian, I wish I could've been loved like Kelsey."

Brian squeezed Sophia hands, "Sophia, I don't know what's happening, but what I feel for you is greater and deeper than anything I could've ever felt for Kelsey."

"Brian, I want to talk about my past on our next date."

"Sophia, are you upset with me?" Brian said, with a concerned expression on his face.

"No, Brian, of course not, I just think too much in one day would be too much for both of us. We'll talk tomorrow, I promise."

After Brian left, Sophia said to the Lord, "Oh Lord please let Brian love me; this man loves with a deep passion, and how I long for someone to love me this way." When Brian got home, the girls ran into his arms and said, "Dad, how did it go?"

"Super!" Brian said with excitement on his face. The girls giggled. When Brian was alone with the Lord he prayed, "Oh Lord, please let Sophia love and forgive me."

Chapter 22

Just before Brian decided to move away from the church that Kelsey attended, he had met three older men, Robert, Enoch, Jacob. Robert was 75, Enoch was 70, and Jacob was 68 years old. Brian had often wondered if these older men were angels disguised as men. In fact, these three men had many of the powers that Satan would later give to Ryan.

The only thing they did not have was the evil eye. Instead they had the third eye, and the Lord allowed them to see the future. They also had the eagle eye, from which they could see what was happening right anywhere in the present. Their most powerful gift though was to transport their bodies to any place they willed them.

Throughout time, the Lord had shown Robert, Enoch, and Jacob the secrets of the universe. They were the great teachers of the past from age to age. They were the masters of wisdom, knowledge, and understanding in the world. They were able to call Jesus to be visible whenever they thought that someone they met needed faith. God knew Brian needed more faith, so He sent these three men into his life.

Brian was glad too when he met them at a supermarket. In less than five minutes, they were praising Brian for taking care of his three daughters. They had talked for an hour in the parking lot of the supermarket. Meanwhile, Brian's daughters were getting restless in the car. Brian had then asked, "How would you guys like to have dinner with us tonight?"

In unison, they had replied, "That sounds super!"

From then on out, every day after work, they were at Brian's house for dinner. Every time they were going to leave after eating dinner, one of Brian's daughters would say, "Please come back tomorrow."

Meanwhile, for some reason Kelsey did not bother Brian while he was friends with Robert, Enoch, and Jacob. The demons did not bother these three men either. Robert, Enoch, and Jacob would go places where even some of the angels feared to go.

In the meantime, Brian finally got his mind off Kelsey. He did not tell the three men about Kelsey because he felt so ashamed. Also, he was afraid they would tell him to stop making love to her. Brian did not like to hurt the Lord, but he enjoyed making love to Kelsey. Unbeknownst to Brian though, the three men knew all about Kelsey and what her assignment was. Yet they did not mention to Brian that they thought he had any weakness. The Lord had taught them through the ages to let Him be the judge. Their main purpose was to encourage Brian. They always came to see Brian as a group of three. It was as if, they were of one body.

One day Brian was talking to Robert, Enoch, and Jacob about the secrets the Lord had revealed to them. He was so surprised at how much God loved humankind. Brian was curious though as to why they never married. They said, "The Lord keeps us happy in His secret place." One of the gifts they said they had been given was to be able to call Jesus any time they wanted to see him. Brian said, "I don't believe you."

So Robert called, "Jesus please show yourself."

Just then Brian's oldest daughter Laquasha said, "Daddy, Jesus is sitting at the table looking at us!" Turning to look, Brian couldn't see a thing. His second daughter, Nadia went over to where the oldest was pointing as if she knew Him too. Jesus smiled and kissed her on her forehead, just before He picked her up. Brian looked at Nadia as she was lifted to a few inches off the chair. Something had picked her up. She was not on the chair but above the seat of the chair, as if someone was holding her. Diane, his youngest, was playing on the floor. She looked at Jesus as if she didn't know him. Brian did not see Jesus because he did not believe then. But he asked Laquasha, "Do you really see Jesus?"

"Yes Daddy."

Brian asked, "How does Jesus look?

"He looks like the pictures hanging on the wall daddy." Jesus appeared to Brian's daughters the way they thought he looked.

Brian asked Laquasha another question, "what is the Lord wearing?"

Laquasha laughed and responded, "A white robe silly."

Brian smiled and said, "Sounds good honey." Robert, Enoch, and Jacob all laughed, and Jesus laughed with them.

Jacob said, "You will see Jesus when you move to your new place. You will also see him whenever you go to heaven, until your faith is built up. Brian looked at the three men with a blank look on his face, as he found that he had nothing to say to such uplifting news. Jesus stayed for a while, and then he vanished.

When Robert, Enoch, and Jacob were about to leave after dinner that night, Diane, the two year old, wanted them to come back again. Brian laughed and said, "One of them will have to do the cooking."

"I will do the cooking," Enoch said with a smile.

Robert continued, "And I will buy the food."

The three men who were visiting then all said together: "We will be here tomorrow at 5 instead of 6 then." Everyone hugged each other before the three men left.

They came over for dinner for the next three weeks. While they were with Brian and his daughters, Brian had such a peace that he could not have described it if he had wished to. Brian noticed that even Kelsey did not bother him. At least, not to his knowledge.

Chapter 23

While Brian was sitting on the bench waiting for his second date with Sophia, he thought about when he first went to confront the pastor and his wife. He remembered making an appointment to see them both, and Kelsey ended up being the only one present. He mentioned the incident to her, and the only thing she said was, "You liked it."

I'm trapped! Brian thought to himself as he walked out of the church office. He did not understand why Ryan, the pastor, didn't meet him too after he had made an appointment to see them. Brian did not know the pastor was a master of leaving his body. Not only was Ryan able to leave his body, but he had learned over the years how to transport his whole body physically. It was not just his spirit and soul, but his flesh and blood body.

Ryan found out that if he would give his life to Satan, many demons would possess his body and give him powers that he'd never dreamed he could have. Ryan was given the gifts of clairvoyance, clairaudience (the ability to hear sounds not normally audible), telekinesis, telepathy, the evil eye, hypnotic suggestion, and crystal gazing (to see into the past or future). Ryan also had the ability to get into someone else's body and use them for whatever reason he wanted. He first had to put them in a trance-like state, and while in it, they had no control over their mind, emotions, or will. Ryan was also able to be in more than one place at a time. The best gift he had was thereby his ability to transport his whole physical body to any place he wanted. He could even go through the walls.

Ryan was thenceforth commanded by Satan to go on an assignment for him. There were two people Satan wanted to destroy: one was Brain and the other was Sophia. Satan manipulated the church to vote for Ryan to be their next pastor. The last pastor had only recently died. Before Ryan became the next pastor though, he worked with the church and gave generous offerings. Ryan was thus there for the church in their time of crisis. He helped the poor, and put several people through college. Satan was the one who told Ryan and Kelsey he wanted them to get married, so that Ryan could have a wife when he pastored Brian's church. Ryan and Kelsey agreed to these terms, because it was in Kelsey's will to please Satan as well. Ryan did not love anyone but himself, but he did like the way Kelsey looked.

Kelsey did not mind marrying Ryan because he had billions of dollars. He was not bad looking either, at 5'11", with a slim body, and a light cream colored complexion. Kelsey had heard he was as good in bed with women as with men. She did not care; as long as he let her be free, to make love to whomever she wished.

In the present, Sophia was growing nervous about the approaching second date. She kept thinking how Brian had loved Kelsey. *How did Kelsey look? Was she beautiful? How did she get Brian to be so much in love with her?* He even wanted to commit himself to a mental institution after Kelsey died. Sophia thought that no man had ever loved her that way. She could love Brian that way, but she wasn't sure he would love her that much back. *Jesus, help me to calm down. Lord, you said everything was going to work out between Brian and me. Father, help me to have peace.* At the same time, Brian did not want Sophia to think less of him either. He liked the feeling that Sophia gave him when she looked at him.

As Brian and Sophia were thinking though, Satan had gathered some of his demons together to try and break up the happy union between Brian and Sophia. "Whisper in Sophia ear and make her feel afraid," he said. At the same time, the Lord told his angels to remind Brian and Sophia to remember what He said, and trust Him.

The demons spoke to Sophia, "Just don't tell Brian anything about your husbands. You've already told him enough. Brian's going to think you're going to leave him like you did with your other three husbands."

Sophia said to herself, *it would be like hiding something from him.* "Lord, what should I do?" Two of Sophia's angels sent a breeze to let Sophia know all was well. Sophia felt it, even though the window was closed. "Where did that breeze come from?" Sophia smiled, "thank you Lord!"

The Lord spoke to Satan, "Don't bother Brian and Sophia anymore; I'm going to give them a time of rest before they face the battles before them." Subsequently, Brian and Sophia decided to have dinner at Sophia's house because she wanted to talk about her past. Brian was so nervous. "Lord, maybe I said too much; Sophia probably thinks I'm a weak person. I shouldn't have told her I wanted to commit myself to a mental institution after Kelsey died. Please help me to calm down." One of Brian's Angels reminded Brian of the Lord's promise to him.

Brian's clothes were informal: a sky blue shirt and blue dungarees. Brian thought his heart would burst out. He was happy, yet scared. He knew what it was to be so happy that he couldn't breathe, and then have his heart broken in a thousand pieces. When he rang the bell, he prayed, "Lord, help me." While Sophia answered the door, she prayed, "Lord help me." The Lord and the four angels started to laugh. The Lord said, "This is their time to be happy."

The door opened, and Sophia stretched out her arms. Brian took Sophia in his arms. Her smell was like the smell of flowers. He smelled like cinnamon rolls. Neither of them ever wanted to let the other go. They looked into each other's eyes and kissed for 15 seconds. Sophia smiled, "come in Brian."

"Don't mind if I do," Brian smiled. After they ate dinner, Brian helped Sophia wash the dishes. "Brian, I think it's time I told you about my three husbands."

"Three husbands," Brian said jokingly. Sophia looked as if she was going to cry. Brian paused for a second, and then without thinking, started laughing. Sophia laughed with him.

"I guess we'd better sit down." Sophia said in a low soft voice. Brian smiled. "Brian, I told you some things about my parents. My mother taught me to never let a man use me. So instead, I would always get married. They would ask to marry me since I wouldn't give in to their sexual pleasure."

"Sophia, that's wonderful, you don't have to tell me anymore."

"Brian, don't you want to know why I divorced them?"

"No! It had to have been their fault anyway."

"Brian! Don't you want to know what my sex life was like in the marriages?"

"Not really." Brian touched her face and said, "Let's get married and I will find out." Brian did not want to know any details about Sophia's sexual past because it would only tempt him to be jealous anyway. His ego wanted to think she had really always wanted him even though she had never met him.

"Brian, aren't you afraid to just marry me, after what happened with you and Susan?"

"Heavens no!

"Why not?"

"Because the Lord told me everything is going to be all right." Brian took Sophia in his arms and kissed her on her face and mouth for one minute. Sophia thought she had died and gone to heaven. Brian's kisses were different than any of her husbands'; it felt as if Brian's life depended on how she responded to him. Brian loved Sophia because she was the first woman he kissed who trembled in his arms. Brian also felt good about Sophia. She was a reality, and he did not have to hide his love for her from the world. Sophia put some romantic music on. They kissed and hugged and danced slow for two hours straight. That very night they decided to get married within the next two weeks.

Chapter 24

After Brian had left the church office, he decided that he had to leave the congregation. Susan was gone; he could not talk to Ryan, because he yielded himself over and over again to Kelsey's temptations. For as much as Brian did not feel the grievance of the Holy Spirit, he began to reason within himself that what he was doing was not wrong, since Kelsey would come through the walls to make love with him. So he did not try to confess to the church every time he and Kelsey had sex anymore. Brian left the church, not because he felt guilty, but because Kelsey refused to divorce Ryan and marry him in honor. Brian was tired of being used every time she wanted to release herself with him.

He knew if he came to the church and said that Kelsey came through locked doors to make passionate love to him, the church would put him in a mental institution. He could not even go to his family, as even his brother Kyle had said it was only demons. The only one that might have believed him would have been his grandmother, who raised him.

Brian would cry for hours on end while his daughters were asleep. One night while Brian was crying, it seemed as if he was no longer there. Brian did not know what was happening. He looked around and there was his body lying on the floor in his bedroom. "Lord, what's happening to me? Am I dead?"

"No, I just want you to be relieved of your pain." Brian felt no pain, only a feeling of peace. Weeks went by and Brian realized that just by thinking it, he could will himself in and out of his body. "He could be anywhere he wanted to go. After a month of experiencing leaving his body, he really began enjoying seeing the spiritual world. Sometimes he would see spirits that were on the Lord's side, and others times he would see spirits that were against Him. The Lord taught Brian how to fight the spirits that were his enemies, to overcome them with the blood of the lamb, and to defeat them with the word.

The Lord spoke to Brian one particular day and said, "Brian, I want to start sending you on missions out of the body. Some people just can't be reached in this world. I will teach you what you should do." Brian smiled and said, "Yes Lord!" Brian was happy and excited with his new life and new experiences with the Lord. Sometimes the Lord would lead Brian to people sitting on a bench, and Brian would tell them about the good news of Jesus Christ. That good news was not only concerning their salvation, but also how Jesus Christ was coming back to set up his government on this earth. It would be a kingdom where His church would be ruling.

Another time when Brian left his body, the Lord led him to a school yard in an urban city. A group of young boys, whose ages were between nine and eleven, were beating up a boy around 8 years old. Brian pulled the boys off the younger child, at which point the boys tried to attack him. Their hands went right through Brian's body. Terrified that Brian was a ghost, they ran away. The young boy's right eye was badly damaged, so Brian put his hand on the boy's right eye, and the boy was healed. The boy touched his eye, and he did not feel any pain. Not knowing what to think, the boy had walked away with a puzzled look on his face.

Brian was excited over this gift that the Lord had given him, as it took his mind off of Susan, and kept him from thinking about Kelsey all day. Most of the time, the Lord would take Brian some place to help someone, or just witness for Him. When Brian was free to go wherever he wanted, he usually willed himself to heaven. "Only in the Lord's presence can I resist Kelsey's temptation." When Brian went to heaven, he would sometimes find himself in front of a huge mansion. On one such occasion, he saw two tall angels standing on each side of the opening of his kitchen, which was adorned at the moment with beautiful hanging plants. He saw Jesus Christ working on the knob of his kitchen cabinet. As Brian stood there looking at the back of Jesus while he worked, he felt all of Jesus' emotions. Jesus acknowledged him for a second and then went back to work on Brian's mansion. Shortly thereafter, Brian found himself back in his body.

Another time when Brian left his body, he cried out, "Jesus, I want to see you!" Brian then found himself in front of a classroom where the Lord was teaching some children. The Lord said to Brian with excitement in His voice, "Hi Brian!"

"Hi!" Brian responded. Jesus came over to Brian and embraced him tightly. Brian felt so much love coming from the Lord while he hugged him. Brian was excited by this, but because he was so emotionally torn up within himself, he did not allow his heart to be open to anyone. He did not ask the Lord why all this was happening to him. The Lord had such happiness and love in his expression, it seemed to Brian that he was in the Lord's presence for ten whole minutes, after which Brian found himself back in his body. Many times thereafter Brian would will himself to heaven to be with the Lord.

One of those days, the Lord said to Brian, "I don't want you to keep coming up here; you should put your mind on winning souls for me." At this, Brian was a little upset, but in the end he trusted the Lord's wisdom. Coming to see Jesus made him forget the daily pain of Susan leaving him, and Kelsey using him.

Even though Brian did not want to let his emotions be free, he couldn't help but feel a certain excitement at seeing Jesus. He loved the Lord, even though he sometimes felt bitter towards Him. He wanted to keep his mind off Kelsey, so he thought about Jesus all day.

Chapter 25

After agreeing upon marriage with Sophia, Brian was more excited than he had ever believed he could be. He got into his car after walking ten minutes from her apartment, and he asked himself, *am I really getting married to someone who actually wants and loves me?* He had just seen Sophia a few minutes ago, and he missed her already. *Maybe I should call Sophia? No, I will see her tomorrow; only two weeks to wait until we marry.* Dwellings on these thoughts, Brian considered one of his favor scriptures: "Don't *be anxious for anything, but do everything with prayer and supplication.*" Brian began to think about the emotions he felt while he was kissing and hugging Sophia, about how he wanted to take her in her bedroom and make love to her. But Brian loved the Lord too much to fail him now. Brian mused, "Curiosity killed the cat." Yet, Brian could not help but wonder if Sophia would resist him if he tried to have sex with her before they were married.

Meanwhile, Sophia was thinking about Brian. *This man knows how to drive a woman crazy with his kisses. How she wanted to just go in the bedroom and give herself totally to him.* Sophia rebuked herself, "Lord help me! When I didn't believe in you, I had more morals than I have now. When I see Brian tomorrow, please help me to put You before myself and him. Maybe it won't be too much of a temptation; after all, we have only been dating officially for a little while. Besides, Brian is taking me out to eat tomorrow, and then we're supposed to go bowling. Maybe after we bowl, Brian will be too tired to come in."

Both of them were restless and could not sleep. Brian wanted to call Sophia but did not want seem too anxious. Meanwhile, Sophia was hoping Brian would call. She did not want him to think she was desperate, so she did not call him. It seemed to take forever before the next day came.

That night was long for both Sophia and Brian; they kept looking at the clock. *Oh God,* they both prayed, *please let this night be over.* Finally, they fell asleep. They both were awoken early in the morning by the sound of rain falling hard outside. The rain sounded to both of them as if it were celebrating their happiness. Sophia was nonetheless a little disappointed because of the storm outside, but she would not let it stop her from shopping for her wedding. Brian and the girls just stayed home and played board games. When evening came, Brian asked his oldest daughter to watch the other girls. The girls were excited because their Dad was happy, so they helped him pick out the clothes he was going to wear that night.

Brian was on time this time, at 7 p.m. sharp. Sophia opened the door. "Well, come in Brian. How are you?"

"Better now," he grinned. "How was your day?"

"Exciting; I was thinking about you all day," Sophia blushed. Brian pulled her close and kissed her something fierce. "Brian!" Sophia breathed, pausing to get her breath, "We'd better get going if we plan on making it to that dinner." Brian smiled at the thought.

While they were having dinner, Brian was wondering if Sophia would wait to get married, or if she would have sex with him if he asked her to. Sophia prayed to herself, *Lord, I know that look; Brian's thoughts are not on you. Help me to say no to him if he asks me to have sex. I wish I did not want him so much, at least not now.*

After the dinner and an inexperienced bowling session, Brian took Sophia home. She stood in front of the door before she opened it for a few minutes. Deep down, Brian did not want to sin against God, but his ego was there. Thinking about how cold Susan had been to him, he wanted to see Sophia's expression when he approached her with a sexy attitude. Brian said, in a low sexy voice, "Aren't you going to let me in sweetheart?"

Sophia said, nervously, "Sure, why not?" As soon as they closed the door, Brian pulled Sophia into his arms and kissed her with a passion like no other. Sophia melted in Brian's arms. "Brian, you're making me so hot."

"I am huh? Well, what should we do about it?" Brian smiled slyly.

"I think we've got to stop this kissing," Sophia replied with a serious look on her face.

Seeing that look humbled his ego, diminishing his thoughts that she might be all over him. Apologetically, he asked, "Sophia, should I go home now?

"No more kissing and touching", she said in a whisper. "Let's play a board game; how about Scrabble?"

"Sounds good to me," Brian smiled, relieved by her reaction. "Sophia, do you mind if I bring my daughters over tomorrow night?"

"Brian, that sounds great; I will make something special for them to eat. Do they like board games?"

"Only more than candy, sweet love." At this, they both started laughing. Later that evening, Brian made his way home.

That night, when Brian went home, he could not sleep. He started to think back when he had first moved to Minnesota. He had been frustrated because it had seemed at times as if the Lord was taking a vacation. Many months had gone by since he'd last heard from the Lord; even though Brian knew He was ever present, this made him restless. Brian did not know how to keep the news of their work to himself. He wanted to tell someone the great things the Lord was doing in the spirit world with him.

After leaving Iowa City, Iowa, Brian had been able to get a teacher position in a small town in Fergus Falls, Minnesota. Brian had left the church he used to attend, and now in his new residence in Minnesota, he had found a new church. Before he made friends in town, he had felt so alone. Eventually though, Brian made friends with other people. He became close to someone in his new residence that he was able to confide in. Travis was the second person Brian told about his experience with the pastor's wife.

Travis was a man open to new ideas and the opinions of others. For reasons like these, Brian praised God for Travis. Brian was at the point of needing someone to believe in what he was going through, and it seemed like the Lord knew he could not bear this alone. Travis quickly became a good friend. Brian could even talk to him about Kelsey, and Travis would not judge him. One of the main reasons Brian thanked God for Travis was that he had believed Brian when he had described how Kelsey had come through the walls and had sex with him. Brain and Travis would pray together that the Lord would deliver Brian, or that the Lord would give Brian what he wanted if it was not against His will.

Things went well for a while for Brain. He and his daughters liked the town, Brian had a good job, and the girls had a good school and daycare. People were more open to Christian in this down, the schools were private and run by Jewish Christians, and Brian had a nice house with a backyard. Brian was happy, and he started to relax with the Lord again. Around this time in his life, he really began to study the bible. He also enjoyed the gift he had of leaving his body.

For years Brian had kept everything about Kelsey to himself, except for what he'd divulged to his half-brother Kyle and his new friend Travis. Even though Brian did not receive any spiritual support from his half-bother, he felt his love. Even though Brian had a friend in his new surroundings, he wanted to see what his new pastor thought about his leaving of the body and working for the Lord in the spirit world. However, the pastor was a little wary at this news, and told Brian not to mention this to anyone in the local church.

Brian eventually had found another friend besides Travis. Ignoring the pastor's advice, he told this new friend about how he could leave the body. Unfortunately, this new friend told someone else, and then the news of Brian leaving his body got back to his pastor. The pastor was upset with Brian because he could not deal with the subject of leaving the body. Consequently, the pastor asked Brian to leave the church. The pastor did not want any division in the church on the subject of leaving the body.

Chapter 26

Meanwhile Satan called a meeting with his demons. "Now is the time to attack Brian; when he is weak."

A demon whispered in Brian's ear, "God doesn't love you; He has forsaken you; He has given you false hope to believe that he wanted to use you for his kingdom. What kind of God are you serving? First, he allowed you to marry a woman who doesn't even like men. Then, he allowed the pastor's wife to go through the walls and force herself upon you sexually. Now, the pastor of your new church thinks you're one of us. All you did was try to confide in this new pastor, but because of his fear of us, he put you out of the church."

Brian then became frustrated with God because he was being tormented by the forces of darkness. Brain was heartbroken, he did not have a wife, and he could not return to the church he had come from because he could not deal with his strong emotions for Kelsey. Brian almost felt forsaken by God because God had been silent in his mind for two months. Whenever he was frustrated, Brian forgot to eat. Many times, his oldest daughter Laquasha would ask him, "Daddy, why don't you eat?"

Brian would reply, "Didn't I eat earlier today?" But the answer was always no. Yet, to please his daughters, he would always make a show of eating something. Sometimes though, Brian would retreat to his room, reading one piece of fiction after another. The pain he felt was against his own weakness. He wanted so much to please God, yet his flesh would cry out to be satisfied by Kelsey. Brian could not even imagine that he would one day find someone else he could love as much as he loved Kelsey.

Whenever Brian was in this depressed state, the Word of God just seemed like words to him. It was very hard for Brian to run to Jesus when he felt so defeated within himself. In this state he was in, The Lord knew He must reach Brian before the demons reached him. So at last, the Lord whispered to Brian to sing to him. Brian heard the Lord say, "Sing Brian." He wanted to be angry with God, but he could not be because he had seen the Lord's goodness every day in his life. As Brain started to sing, he heard many voices accompanying him in perfect harmony.

Brian's daughters came into the room where Brian was and asked, "Daddy where is all that beautiful music coming from?"

Brain responded joyfully, "It is the Lord's angels glorifying God with me." The Lord smiled.

Meanwhile in the present, Brian's daughters were growing excited about going on a date with their dad. They liked Sophia because she had this way of always making them feel included. She knew the right smile to use when the girls looked at her, and she had the right touch. She might only brush them with a hand as lightly as the breeze of a gentle wind, but that feeling was a comfort they couldn't explain.

Brian was supposed to meet Sophia at five; however, he had just gotten home from work at four. "Girls, get a move on, it's nearly 4:20, and it takes at least 45 minutes to get to Sophia's house." Brian had rented an apartment to stay in until their marriage; it was leased month to month. He had taken two months' vacation and come to see Sophia in New York City. After Brian parked his car, he and his daughters walked three blocks to Sophia's house.

As Sophia was waiting for Brian and his daughters, she felt a little relief that the girls were coming with him. "At least while the children are here we won't be tempted to sin against the Lord." Just then the doorbell rang. "Just a minute," she said, before she opened the door. "Well, hello everyone, come on in." Everyone hugged each other, as if their completeness had been restored. "Have a seat," Sophia smiled.

Before Brian spoke, he was a little hesitant because of the delicious smell, "I was wondering Sophia if you would like to go out to eat?"

"Brian, I made a meal for the girls." Sophia said with a happy smile on her face.

"Well, in that case, I suppose we could spoil them just this once." Brian replied with a grin. While everyone was eating, Brian asked, "Girls, do you want to stay in and play a board game, or go someplace else?

Laquasha said, "Dad, let's go shopping."

But her younger sister Nadia disagreed, saying, "I don't want to go shopping daddy."

Sophia said, "Now Laquasha, when we first met I took everyone shopping, while daddy stayed home and took a nap. Maybe we should try doing something else together this time?"

"Yes, that's fine," she said in a low voice.

Brian was looking at Nadia and Diane, "So girls, where would you like to go?" He then looked at Sophia, "what time is it?"

Sophia looked at her watch. "It's 6:15 already."

Brian turned back to his girls, "Alright then, have you decided where you want to go?"

They looked at each other smiling, and announced together in unison, "To the zoo!"

After they came back from the zoo, everyone sat down and played Monopoly. It was midnight when Brian and the girls finally went home. From the evening's events, Sophia was both sad and happy. She wanted to be alone with Brian, yet not alone, because she was afraid of the desires within herself. Every time she was around Brian she just wanted to go in the bedroom and make love to him. Brian however did not have Sophia on his mind, as he was generally occupied with his daughters. Consequently, it didn't really hit him until he had returned home and put his daughters to bed.

"I didn't even kiss Sophia goodnight." So Brian decided to call her.

"Hello?" Sophia answered in a sleepy voice.

"Hi sweetheart, I'm sorry to call you so late. I forgot to kiss you goodnight."

"Aww Brian, thank you so much for calling. I was feeling sort of down in my spirit when we didn't get our traditional goodbye."

Brian said, "Well, kiss kiss cutie, I love you. Would you like to go someplace tomorrow just the two of us?"

Sophia replied, "That sounds wonderful; we'll decide tomorrow when you get here? Around seven? Kiss kiss Brian, I love you too."

Before Brian felt asleep, his mind began to wonder again to back before he left Ryan and Kelsey's church. Because he had wanted to be in right standing with God, Brian had been willing to tell the whole church that he was sinning against Him. Since he'd never done anything like this before, he didn't exactly know how to go about it. Eventually, he'd decided that when it was time for the people at church to testify to the goodness of God, he would openly confess that he had committed adultery. When he'd followed through with that plan, Brian remembered how the church had become silent; one could have heard the creeping of a mouse if there had been one bold enough to do so in that place. For the sake of propriety, Brian did not say who he had committed adultery with. Brian felt that was God's business, and not that of the congregation. After this moment in his life, the people that were under Pastor Ryan and his wife treated Brian with disrespect. It did not matter to Brian how they treated him because all he wanted was to be free from the bondage of Kelsey's intrusions into his bedroom. Although Brian continued to yield to Kelsey when she came to bedroom, he felt he now had a right to praise God because he'd tried to confess his sin to the church.

Satan continued to say to Brian, "God has not forgiven you for sinning, even though you confess, you continue to sin."

"Yes," said Brian, "but I am free to praise the Lord!" Meanwhile, Satan continued to accuse Brain before the throne of God. The Lord's Angels would whisper to Brian to forsake his present situation. Brain remembered how much he wanted to please the Lord, but his flesh overcame him, affecting him more than his spiritual need to love and please God. Then bitterness would justify his behavior. He did not like being rejected by his wife. He remembered with pain trying to show affection to Susan, though all he received in return was a disgusted look.

When Brian saw Kelsey, his whole body became alive. All she had to do was smile at him. Every time he would smile at her, before the week was over, she would come through his locked doors naked. Brain yielded to every precious fruit she presented. As he laid there thinking, he remembered how even when he left the church where he was raised, he was still pursued by the pastor's wife through her projected spirit. Kelsey knew Brian would not yield himself to her anymore when she came through closed doors. So Kelsey projected thoughts to Brian to meet her somewhere else to have sex.

Kelsey would use telepathic abilities, and leave her body to talk to Brian while he was asleep. Brian would get up in a trance and call Kelsey on the phone. She would talk to him in the trance and tell him to meet her at a hotel. Before Brian called Kelsey on the phone, he would lose all memories of who he was. Because Brain was so in love with Kelsey, it was easy for her to control his mind in this way. Many times Brain found himself in a room making love to Kelsey. It seemed as if he was in a trance. In this trance, he did not seem to have his own will. Brain did not understand why the Lord allowed Kelsey to continue to use him. Despite all this, Kelsey was unsatisfied with Brian's lack of will when she made love to him. So Kelsey decided to wake Brian out of the trance-like state; though she did not know that the Lord moved upon her to do so. The Lord wanted Brian to have his own free will.

That night, while Kelsey was making love to Brian in a trance-like state, she used hypnotic suggestions on him to wake him out of her trance. When he came to, Brian was quite distraught in his reaction to Kelsey: "Kelsey, you can't come against my will, unless you marry me, you must leave me alone!" Kelsey tried several times to use Brain and then wake him up in this way, each time hoping to find him enjoying himself.

But when Kelsey saw that Brian was determined to marry her, she finally said, "Okay. I will marry you in the spirit world." This caused Brian to become furious with Kelsey; he jumped out of the bed and hit the wall with his fist.

"Marry you in the spirit?!" He screamed, and felt that he was losing his mind. "I want to marry you in the physical world, with honor. Unless you divorce your husband, you really must leave me alone!"

Kelsey touched Brian softly, "I have been divorced from my husband for several years now. I just didn't tell you until now because the church must never find out. We've always taught the congregation against divorce." Kelsey started to rub Brian's arm, but Brain pulled his arm away in anger.

"No, not until we marry," Brain said lowering his voice. Kelsey smiled at Brian, "so you agree to marry me in the spirit?" Brian looked at Kelsey with a puzzled look, "Yes." At that, Kelsey disappeared through the walls with a smile.

As Brian laid there on the bed, he remembered crying out to God to help him. "Lord, please help me. I don't know what I'm doing anymore. I just agreed to marry Kelsey in the spirit world." A month later, he received a copy of her divorce papers in the mail. Brain hadn't seen Kelsey in the flesh and blood since he had moved away from the church where she and her husband had presided.

Brian didn't hear anything back from the Lord. Yet, he knew the Lord was with him. Brian's heart was filled with happiness. *At least I won't be in sin anymore*, he thought. The next evening, Brian was taken out of his trance again in a hotel. "How did I get here, Kelsey?"

"I projected thoughts for you to meet me here."

"Who are all the people in this room?" Brian asked nervously.

Kelsey replied, "These are the people who will witness our marriage in the spirit world, and this man is the pastor who will marry us." There were twelve other people present, all in a trance. Brian could have little objection, even if he had wanted to. After they were married, Kelsey kissed Brian and said, "I'll be seeing you very soon."

Kelsey's ex-husband Ryan soon found out that Kelsey had married Brian in the spirit world. He was more furious with Kelsey than at the thought that she was falling in love with Brian. This was the reason he had divorced Kelsey several years ago. "What if he tells someone?!" Ryan screamed at Kelsey.

Kelsey said, "Oh don't worry about your money and reputation. You're afraid you are going to lose and that makes you unsettled. Most people would think Brian were crazy if he said he'd married me in the spirit world."

"Why didn't you counsel with me first?' Ryan said, with hate in his expressions. Kelsey looked at him with a grin, "You never counseled me when you went to Susan's bed. What a rotten thing to do, to impregnate Susan with your child. The poor woman is already messed up, so why mess her up more?"

Ryan replied with a calm voice, "When did you become so holy and sanctified?"

Kelsey said in anger, "The point is, why I should consult you for anything?!"

Ryan responded with returned anger, "I'm running this show, so you'd better watch yourself before we all are exposed!" Kelsey was sick to her stomach when she thought back to her agreement with Satan to marry Ryan. She thought, *why could I not have met Brian before I got involve with Satan? I love the way Brian loves me. I know deep down he still loves the Lord too. But what are my chances of ever being free of Satan, and loving the Lord like he loves God?* Kelsey walked away from Ryan, but she did not take the chance to see Brian again in the spirit until things had cooled down between her and Ryan.

For two weeks Brian was frustrated because Kelsey didn't show or give any sign to let him know what was going on. Then, on one random Tuesday, she was back again. Brian awoke to her just lying there, naked in his bed, holding onto his private parts. "How dare you come to me whenever you feel like having some release? Where have you been for the past two weeks?"

"Around," she said as she stroked his shoulder gently.

"Where?! In someone else's bed?!" he snapped bitterly, flinching away from her touch.

"Brian, we're married now. I wouldn't make love to anyone but you," she smiled.

"I don't believe you. How could you marry me and disappear without a word for two weeks? I'm tired of this. You have to marry me in the natural way, where everyone will know we're married. I want a marriage certificate from the state.

"Brian, I told you I can't. Many souls might even leave Jesus if they found out that we're married. How much more so if I married you before the whole church? Ryan and I told the members that they couldn't marry twice. Many of them even left happy second marriages, simply because they trusted my ex-husband and I that it was God's will. Sweet baby, let's just enjoy ourselves. I promise you from now on, I will be in your bed every night."

"I want to see you, not just in my bed; I want you to be a mother to my girls." Brian sat up and ran his hand through his hair. Kelsey leaned over to him; the smell of her perfume was intoxicating; the touch of her soft hands melted him. Eventually, he succumbed to her calls. The next day, after leaving the hotel Kelsey had brought him to, Brian headed home. His daughters were of course glad as always to have him back. Thereafter, Kelsey kept her word for the next six months. She was in his bed every night.

That night when Brian came home to his daughters, he started to cry out to the Lord, "Help me! Help me! Oh Lord! Speak to me! I don't know what to do!" At truly his lowest hour, Brian felt a cool breeze as he cried out to the Lord. A calm feeling came over him, and he began to experience peacefulness. Brian heard the Lord speak to him.

"Brian, I want you to understand there is a battle going on between Satan and me, and I am allowing him to come against your will. Together, I want to show Satan that we will win against all the manipulating evil he is trying to inflict on us by using Kelsey. I will show Satan that no matter what he does to try and destroy you and Kelsey; I will win in the end. Brian, I do not see you in sin when Kelsey puts you in a trance; when you're not aware of what is happening to you. But when when you are aware of this sin, I want you to fight against such evil, which is why I made Kelsey wake you out of the trance. I want you to try and win her to me"

After much thought, Brian was finally able to fall asleep, long after leaving Sophia's house that night. Brian woke up the next day thinking, *Sophia and I will be married in three days. Lord, help me to wait until then before we make love. You have been so good to me, and I don't want to hurt you again just to satisfy myself.*

Sophia was also talking to the Lord that morning, "Father you have been so good to me. I don't want to put Brian before you, and I definitely don't want to put myself before you." Brian arrived at Sophia's apartment at around seven that evening. While Brian was waiting for Sophia to finish getting ready, he noticed for the first time how beautiful her furniture was. She'd had it all shipped from Greece; the colors were sky blue and white. The carpet matched the furniture and walls, and Brian liked the taste. After all, his favorite color was any shade of blue.

The two of them decided to go to a Broadway play. During the show, Brian put his arm around Sophia, but she did not want to kiss anymore until they were married. After it was over, Brian told Sophia that he should probably go home. He told her that he would have a hard time keeping his hands off of her if he didn't.

As Brian waited for tomorrow to come, he thought about Kelsey and how he had tried to resist her when she came to him in the spirit world. On that particular evening, Brian was not yet asleep, but about to fall asleep. Kelsey was standing by his bed smiling. Brian said, "No, Kelsey, no, the Lord said that what we are doing is wrong."

"Who cares what He says?" Kelsey said in a whisper, Brian snapped at her,

"I care; don't you have any fear of God?"

As Kelsey walked through the walls in anger, she screamed, "Forget you, I didn't want you anyway."

As time went on, Brian missed Kelsey and wanted her even more since he had refused her. He was very frustrated, feeling as if he just could n't have any happiness. "The Lord doesn't want me to will myself to heaven anymore; I don't have a wife; why can't I have this little happiness with Kelsey?"

After a short while, Kelsey continued to come to him. "No!" he would say. "No, Kelsey, the Lord said no!" However, he wanted her even though he was supposed to say no. Every time Kelsey came to Brian, she had sex with him, and Brian received her. He did not know what else he could do.

That very night, while Brian was complaining about his situation, his half-brother Kyle called. Kyle told him that Kelsey was holding a retreat free for anyone who wanted to get away to the country. Brian was so happy to hear this news that he decided to call Kelsey at his old church. Kelsey answered the phone. "Hello, Kelsey speaking!"

"Good morning Kelsey, this is Brian."

"Good morning Brian; how may I help you?' Kelsey spoke to him as if he was a stranger.

"Kelsey, how are you? The tone of Brian's voice was that of a friend.

"I'm on my post for the Lord." Kelsey said in a sanctified tone. Brian was too excited to notice Kelsey's coldness towards him.

"I heard about the retreat, and I think I will be attending; I plan on bringing my daughters with me."

After a long pause, Kelsey finally replied in a whisper, "That's great Brian."

"Well, have a good day Kelsey; I will see you at the retreat," Brain said with a cheerful spirit. But Kelsey did not respond to anything else that Brian said because she had mixed emotions; she just hung up the phone and sat there thinking. She wanted to see him, yet she was afraid the church might see her emotions. She definitely did not want the church members to see Brian's emotions.

One day Satan himself spoke to Brian. "You are damned. Why do you continue to teach your children about God? Why do you pray to God to fight for you? Why continue to praise God and read the Bible when you don't obey it?"

In response, Brian started singing, "I will praise him in Hell because He is worthy of my praise." At this, the Lord and some of the angels around Brian started laughing.

Satan then spoke to his demons, "We must cause Brain more suffering. He is not letting up on praising God." Satan wasn't the only one who was about to turned against Brian, God was determined to be first in Brian life; even If He had to show His wrath against Brian.

The Lord was looking down at what was taking place with Brian and Kelsey on the phone, and He thought back to when He had given Brian the gift to leave his body. Notably, Brian had not tried to use the gift to see Kelsey in the spirit world. All he wanted to do was see Him. The Lord recalled how Brian was so excited, and how he would call out to Him and say, "Lord I want to see you."

One of the angels spoke, "Lord, I know you won't put more on Brian than he can bear." Some of the angels felt sad for Brian, and were worried about his future. They had seen how Brian wanted to do right, and how he tried to praise the Lord no matter what he suffered. Most of all, they saw how he taught his daughters to love and fear the Lord.

The Lord said, "I'm allowing Brian to go on this retreat. I want him to be hurt by Kelsey. Even though Brian loves me, he must understand true love is to love even if there is no love in return. He must understand that true love is not selfish. Kelsey only thinks about satisfying her own flesh, and I want Kelsey and Ryan to be exposed at this retreat. Eventually, Ryan is going to die of a sickness that no pain medicine will be able to relieve. All of his money will not do him any good. Kelsey will be helpless, and without any power with the local congregation. She will not be able to take the pressure of what others are thinking when Brian's love for her becomes obvious."

Some time after Brian got off the phone with Kelsey, while lying in bed, he continued to think about the past. He remembered how he and the girls had attended their old church before he had left. At the time, an ambivalent force pulled him both toward and away from the place, torn between his love for God and Kelsey. All Brian wanted to do now was see Kelsey face to face where other people could see them together.

The next morning, Brian and the girls packed the car and headed for the church retreat. Naturally the girls were excited, but Brian was even more so. His heart felt as if it could burst.

Meanwhile, God was talking to some of the angels about the situation: "Brian is about to be delivered from Kelsey. Judgment will fall on her and her ex-husband. I will allowed Ryan to provoke Me so much that it will be one of the reason that hasten my return. Because Brian has continued to disobey me, I am going to work out his disobedience for his own good. He will be crushed like he has never been crushed before, and he will need my help. However, he won't call out for my help; instead, he will want to commit himself to an institution. I have two prayer warriors whom Brian will meet. I will have my servants who love me bear him up in prayer."

The angels were concerned about Brian's dilemma. "Lord, we know you won't give Brian more than what he can bear." The Lord spoke, "It's all going to work out for the good." In truth though, the Lord was sad because of Brian's pain and frustration.

Chapter 27

Satan presented himself to the Lord before the throne of God. There, he asked God, "Why do you continue to work with Ryan and Kelsey, when all they do is plan on how to destroy souls?" The Lord knew Satan was right to speak out against Ryan and Kelsey, because they did not have any fear of Him. The Lord felt a strong anger within Himself. How many times did He plead with Ryan and Kelsey to love Him, and to feed His sheep? All they did was use their gifts to satisfy their own lusts. They would use His blood as their defense over and over. The Lord did love them; oh, how He loved them. It would not hurt Him so much if they had just sinned, but Ryan and Kelsey used their gifts to destroy His sheep.

The Lord started to cry when he thought about how Ryan and Kelsey had used Brian and Susan. The Lord did not judge Susan for having her last baby by Ryan. He had forced Susan into a trance and raped her. Ryan and Kelsey had been in a position to teach Susan how to love her husband. They knew why Susan turned to women to love. All Ryan and Kelsey did was take advantage of the marriage, but it made Susan bitter against the Lord of glory. Not only did Ryan rape Susan, but he did not use his gifts to help souls to believe in God's might. After all of that trauma, Susan felt hopeless, and she could not trust anyone anymore.

Year after year, the Lord had sent people to Kelsey and her husband. He was thinking about how Ryan and Kelsey refused to listen to Him; how they treated Him as if He were stupid. The Lord continued to remember how they would use His Word to be forgiven of their sins, as they continued to do evil without godly sorrow. God would yield to them though; His blood would wash them clean because of the faith they had that He would forgive them.

After thinking about Ryan and Kelsey, the Lord spoke to some of his angels. "Now I'm going to laugh at Ryan and Kelsey. Even though Ryan will be sick, he will still be able to leave his body to do Satan's evil. The Lord told his angles, "When anything is harming the body, a person's spirit will usually come back to it as a protective measure. Ryan, however, is an exception. Satan will be laughing at Ryan, while using his spirit to continue his evils. It will seem like the church is overcome by the power Satan gives to this man, as he assists in the genocide of millions of Christians; but I will win at the end. Kelsey will be helpless, and without any power over the true church. When Brian comes around her, she will be under pressure, and afraid that the people will see the love she feels for Brian in the expression on her face. It will feel to Brian as if Kelsey has put a sword through his heart. Even though Brian loves Me, he is madly in love with her. Kelsey can't take the pressure of being rejected by the church because of her own personal weaknesses. Brian has never been treated this way by Kelsey in public, and when his hopes are dashed, he will be ever so crushed." The Lord spoke with an angry voice, but with sadness in his eyes.

As time went on, The Lord wept as Brian became weaker and weaker in spirit. Yet, He always found comfort in Brian's faithfulness to praising and worshipping him in every situation. In some ways then, The Lord was very pleased with Brian; no matter how much pressure he was under, Brian always taught his children about the goodness of the Lord. Still, it hurt the Lord when Brian would become isolated for hours in his room without speaking to anyone. The Lord would often remind Brian to sing to Him, and Brian would sing, and the depressing demon would always run. Sometimes, when Brian would isolate himself, the Lord would remind him to eat something. Brian knew he could not allow himself to die because he had his girls to look after. He wanted earthly love so badly. Many times, the Lord would speak to Brian when he wanted love, whispering in his ear, "so do I, Brian. Please love me." The Lord understood why Brian was so depressed though, as the only love he'd ever really felt from a woman was from Kelsey.

The Lord spoke to some of his angels. "I must reach Brian. He must understand that true love goes to the Creator first. Then, Brian will be able to love the way I want him to love, not just to satisfy his lust but to give one hundred percent to Me. By giving himself totally to Me, he will be able to give himself completely to someone else. Brian must see that Kelsey is only concerned about her own satisfaction, and doesn't know how to love Me or anyone else. She doesn't even know how to love herself. To love the self is to give all of one's self for the rescue of someone else."

The Lord was hurt by Kelsey, whom He loved, but her heart was so hardened against Him that she did not hear His voice anymore. All Kelsey wanted to do was get what she could from the Lord. She used every means to get it, whether it was by satisfying her lust or abusing those who came against her. She wanted to see Brian fall, not because she hated him, but because she knew Brian was in love with God. She felt guilty because she knew there was no excuse for her not to love Him too, but she just couldn't let go of the pain He had allowed her to experience. The hurt in her heart was all she knew, and she didn't know how to get through it.

Chapter 28

It was only two more days before Brian and Sophia would be married; so they decided to take Brian's daughters sightseeing. The girls were thrilled to see so many things that they had never seen before. New York City was an exciting place to visit, but Brian would not want to live in the city forever. He and Sophia had talked about moving back to Minnesota, and Sophia had willingly approved of the move. But Brian's thoughts were still caught up in the past.

The Lord had tried hard to reach Kelsey. He loved her and Ryan no less than anyone else in His flock. He understood Kelsey's sad childhood of passing from home to home, and The Lord knew that all Kelsey wanted now was love and acceptance. The Lord spoke to her many times trying to win her love, but she did hear the Lord speaking to her soul, as she generally fought her inner thoughts. After a while though, she began to consider following her heart again, and thereby repenting to the church and marrying Brian.

While Kelsey was considering this notion, Satan saw her weakness and began to speak to her: "Get what you can get out of life; you only live once. You don't want to be disgraced by repenting and confessing that you're not a holy woman." As was often the case, Kelsey's heart turned to stone at the sound of The Devil's words.

"Why should I trust any God who never cared about me?" she said spitefully.

But this time the Lord answered back: "How many times did I protect you from being raped, when you were moved from home to home as a child? I have never stopped loving you since then Kelsey."

Nonetheless, all Kelsey wanted to do was get what she could get from the Lord, whether it was to satisfy her lust or to abuse anyone who came against her. Kelsey became the meaning of her name, a beautiful island all to itself. The Lord cried and then He became angry. Reluctantly, He spoke to some of the angels, "I think it is time for Kelsey's final judgment. She won't die right away, but by the end, she will wish to. This is the way things must be." The Lord also thought to himself, *All I wanted for Kelsey and Ryan was happiness, but when* they *abuse others they are abusing me too. They are hurting so many innocent souls, all of which are there for their protection.* The angels looked on as the tears of the Lord flowed into the world.

The reason Kelsey was giving a retreat for the congregation was because she felt that the church was falling apart. She needed her status with the church because it made her feel important when the members asked her to pray for them. The members were insecure; with the way things were headed in the world, those who believed in Jesus Christ might soon be dyeing for their faith. Their lives were being threatened by a society that did not want to believe in anything or anyone who said they were wrong.

Every day was heaven for Brian as he packed his bags for the retreat. Brian could not rest, as he thought about Kelsey day and night. Brian was so excited; the closer he came to Kelsey, the happier he became. Even though Brian was married to Kelsey in the spirit world, he had never been satisfied with that. Besides, he felt that the Lord was displeased with him. Brian was hoping Kelsey would marry him now in the honorable way. Brian wanted to please the Lord, and he wanted to see Kelsey in the flesh. He could not even imagine what it would be like to be around her again without any worry of what others were thinking. It never came into Brian's mind that Kelsey would worry what the others thought; he did not realize that she wanted praise form others so badly that she was willing to sacrifice anything to get it.

Brian's daughters were happy too, though they still didn't know what was going on in their father's life. The oldest daughter was nine years old when they had left Kelsey's church; the others were only four and two. Five years had passed since then. He knew the church did not know that he and Kelsey were married, but he thought that Kelsey would be just as happy to see him as he would be to see her.

But Kelsey's ex-husband was dying in the hospital, and the church was unstable about the leadership now. More than ever, she wanted to impress the members of her congregation.

When Brian arrived at the retreat with his daughters he could barely contain his excitement. He had not seen Kelsey in the flesh since he'd left, and even though Brian did not want to hurt Kelsey, he was tired of hiding. So a thought came into his mind: *go show yourself to Kelsey boldly and tell her how much you love her. Tell others you love her too.* Brian didn't recognize the malevolent tone of Satan's voice.

Deep down, Brian was angry with Kelsey for tempting him to sin against the Lord before she married him in the spirit world, and it was hard for him to bear the pain he caused the Lord just to please his own flesh. He hated to hide in secrecy; he wanted everyone to know he loved Kelsey. In his subconscious mind, he wanted to show her that he was man enough pursue her, even though the congregation would be against it. Therefore, when Satan spoke to Brian, it was easy to yield. What The Devil did not know was that God also wanted Brian to show himself to Kelsey.

Across the lawn, Kelsey was talking to some people about Ryan. She was telling them the pastor was too sick to be with them on their retreat. At last, Brian and his girls saw her. As Kelsey was speaking to some of the members, one of Brian's daughters said, "Dad, there she is." His daughters were very happy to see Kelsey, because their dad had always told them that he wanted to go and visit the old church so they could see her again. With a deep breath, Brian walked over to Kelsey and said, "Praise the Lord everyone, how is everybody doing?!"

One woman recognized him and said, "Is that you, Brother Brian? Oh, it's so nice to see you again!" The lady hugged Brian. The church members always called each other by their first names; it was good to be back.

Brian looked at Kelsey with a smile full of love and said, "How are you Kelsey?" He remembered going up to her with a warm smile and trying to embrace her. But Kelsey pushed him away, as if he were a stranger with a bad smell. She then continued to talk with some of the other members as if

Brian was not even there. Brian would never forget what his heart felt at that moment. He felt as if she had stabbed him with a knife. Brian wanted to introduce his daughters to her, but Kelsey looked at him with such scorn that he just walked away.

Seeing his sadness, Brian's older daughter said to him, "Dad, let's go home." Brian put his arms around her and walked away. Brian did not express his feeling to his daughters as he drove back to the hotel. He felt hurt, but he brushed it aside and thought, *maybe I will speak to her when she's not so busy.* He was just so glad to see her, even thinking about being near her for two weeks made his hurt go away. Over the next few days, every time Brian would see Kelsey, she would try to avoid him. This went on for almost a whole week; all the while, Brian's daughters pleaded with their dad to leave.

Pulling his thoughts away from Kelsey for a moment, Brian thought back to when he met Jocko, an ex-warlock. The first time they saw each other was at the very same retreat that Kelsey had scheduled for congregation building. While there, Jocko had told him how he had given his life to Jesus Christ, but still continued to practice witchcraft.

As Brian was sitting on the grass relaxing, one of the members came up to him and asked, "What are you doing?"

"Oh just sitting and thinking," Brian said.

"Thinking about Kelsey?" the man asked.

"Yes!" Brian said in a sad voice.

"She certainly did have some nerve to use you all those years, and now under pressure, she acts as if she doesn't even know you."

Brian was a little surprised; he did not think anyone knew about what was happening with him and Kelsey. "How did you know?" Brian asked.

The man smiled, "The name's Jocko; and I know because I was once a practicing warlock. I gave myself to the Lord Jesus Christ, but I'm not quite delivered yet. Sometimes I fall back into witchcraft because it makes me feel powerful. Believe me, Ryan and Kelsey are some of the top witches and warlocks that work with Satan. Their whole purpose is to destroy the saints." Jocko said.

"Kelsey is a selfish person. She doesn't care who she hurts." Brian said in an angry voice. What Brian did not know though was that Jocko wasn't himself in this moment, as Ryan inhabited Jocko's body. Even though Ryan's body was in the hospital, he was still able to leave in spirit. Ryan was not concerned about Kelsey, but he knew Brian was right in what he said about her, because Ryan was just as selfish as she was. Ryan was already furious with Brian for marrying Kelsey in the spirit world while he was in a trance, and now he had an excuse to abuse Brian.

Jocko told Brian how Satan had alarmed his demons when Jocko had given himself to Jesus Christ, though he'd never truly abandoned his dark practices. What Jocko didn't know was that Satan had also said to his demons, "We will use Jocko when he falls. Ryan will speak through Jocko to confuse Brian."

Some of the congregation also noticed how Kelsey treated Brian so coldly, and they began to wonder why. One of the brothers named Jocko said to some of the congregation, "that's because they're lovers." He said in a sarcastic way.

Brian went to sleep that same night feeling down in his spirit. In the middle of the night, Brian found himself in a trance like state. There was his former pastor Ryan, and before Brian could say anything, Ryan kicked him on his legs repeatedly. Ryan screamed, "Don't speak badly about Kelsey!"

When he found a moment to breath, Brian said, "Why should you care, you're not even married to her anymore?" Ryan started to kick Brian again. Brian screamed out, "I rebuke you evil spirit in Jesus' name." At that, Ryan looked at Brian with a bewildered look, and disappeared. Brian woke up the next morning with bruises on both of his legs. The bruises were so severe that he had a hard time walking, but Brian made himself have faith and claim his healing with the words, "I am healed by the stripes of Jesus Christ. Brian's legs cleared up in a matter of seconds, and he did not feel any more pain.

Chapter 29

The Lord spoke to one of his angels. "Speak in Kelsey's ear. Tell her to repent." Kelsey was in deep thought. She knew she had hurt Brian earlier that day. She almost wanted to cry because she hated herself for being the way she was.

While Kelsey was in deep thought, an angel whispered in the wind, "Repent, Kelsey, repent." She wanted to do so, but did not know how to repent.

Witnessing this, Satan told his demons, "Make sure Kelsey does not repent." While Kelsey sat still after the angel whispered in her ear to repent, she did not know what to do. She dared not even trust God. She had tried to trust people through the years, only to be rejected again and again.

After Kelsey had hurt Brian, he felt that his heart had been torn in a thousand pieces. He started to feel strong emotion against the Lord. "Why can't the Lord let me have some happiness? I can't will myself to heaven, and I can't make love to Kelsey. Lord knows I can't even fall in love with other women. Yet, I can't get Kelsey off my mind. Lord, Help me! Help me! I just can't stand anymore of this. Help me!"

A demon spoke in Brian's ear. "Where is your God now? He doesn't care about your pain. Why do you keep serving him? Curse God and die." That night Brian was emotionally torn, and the tears would not stop. All he could do was cry quietly. "Please Lord no more pain, no more pain!" Brian did not know what to do with all this love he felt for Kelsey. So the Lord spoke to His angels to comfort Brian. While he was crying, he felt a blanket of warmth surround his whole body. He felt such calmness in his spirit.

Brian's daughters did not bother to ask their dad what was wrong. They knew he was hurt by Kelsey's coldness towards him. Their dad had always talked about her to them. After that meeting at the retreat, Brian's daughters did not like Kelsey because she had made their father so sad. After Brian flew home with the girls, that same night, Kelsey came to him through the walls. Brian screamed at her and said, "If you ever bother me again I will blow your head off with a shotgun." And at that, Kelsey ran away. In truth, she was still afraid of dying.

Chapter 30

It was just one more day before Sophia and Brian would be married. *Finally, life will be a reality,* Brian thought. Brian's daughters were also excited. Only the younger daughter Diane would play a part in the wedding ceremony. She would be the flower girl. Sophia did not make Laquasha a bridesmaid because she did not plan to have a big wedding. Of course, Nadia was too young to be a bridesmaid, as she was only nine.

Meanwhile, Brian old church was in need of strong leaders, as their pastor Ryan's body was sick with pain. The doctors could not find medication to take the pain away. The church did not understand why the Lord did not hear their prayers to heal their pastor. Most of all, there was a rumor that the United States might soon be merging its government with that of The New United Nations, and they were not sure how this merger would affect them as Christians.

Therefore, when Kelsey saw Brian, she almost fainted. *Oh no, not now Brian,* she thought to herself. Yet, when Brian called her on the phone, she was happy to hear from him. She wanted to see him, but she did not know how she would react when she did.

Furthermore, Kelsey did not know the demons were attacking her mind. One of them whispered in her ear, "What would the people think if Brian embraced you? You would be a disgrace, especially now that your ex-husband is sick." Kelsey wanted so much to be accepted as someone high and lifted up in the eyes of people. She wanted the saints to see her as a strong woman who didn't even let a man hug her.

Kelsey thought, *Now Brian knows the rules of the church. The men are not supposed to hug the women, and the women are not supposed to hug the men. So why should I show myself to be unholy?* But after Brian left with such hurt in his eyes, Kelsey wanted to call out to him. Her pride would not let her though. She wanted to speak to his daughters because he always talked about them to her, but she also didn't want to hurt him that badly.

Chapter 31

Sophia had been out of her coma for six months. She loved Brian's daughters, and they loved her too. In the six months since she'd known him, Brian and Sophia had communicated on the phone and in spirit. As the wedding had drawn closer, Brian had sent wedding invitations to his family. Only his mother, his half-brother Kyle, and Kyle's family came. Brian's friend Travis also came to the wedding. Sophia sent invitations to her family too, but only Sophia's mother and father accepted them. When the two of them came to the wedding, they were not too excited about Sophia becoming a Christian, and definitely not excited about her marrying one. Nevertheless, they felt good about Brian and his three daughters.

Things were happening so fast for Brian and Sophia. Sophia had only been out of her coma for a few months now, and Kelsey had only been dead for a year. It seemed to Brian that life had turned around. *This is real*, Brian thought; *No more hiding*. His daughters were happy, and they took to Sophia as if they had known her all their lives.

Sophia thought to herself, *why is the Lord so good to me?* She was in love with Brian, and crazy about his girls. This wedding was truly going to be different. She had found her Savior and friend Jesus, and both she and Brian loved the Lord. They knew where they were going because the Lord had revealed to them their purpose.

The wedding took place in a small church in New York City. It seated around 200 people. Brian's girls looked so beautiful in their new dresses. The oldest daughter looked like Brian with curly black hair; she was now fourteen years old. The second daughter was nine, and she looked more like Brian's first wife Susan. Her hair was a light brown. The youngest daughter looked different than the other two, as she had reddish brown hair. She was now seven years old, and had the opportunity to be the flower girl at their wedding.

Brian beamed with pride as his daughter walked down the aisle throwing flowers on the ground. His heart felt as if it was going to burst with happiness when Sophia followed, wearing her long, flowing white gown. Brian was wearing a simple black tuxedo with a white shirt underneath. His outfit was tied together with a simple black bowtie.

The ceremony lasted just over an hour, and was the closest thing to perfection that either of them had ever experienced. Afterwards, the reception was held in one of the enormous ballrooms in the Ritz Carlton, a luxury hotel in downtown New York. After a night of hustle and bustle, the girls were left with a caretaker in Fergus Falls, Minnesota, while Brian and Sophia went on their honeymoon to Sweden for a month.

While Brian and Sophia were away, many changes were taking place in the world around them, especially in the United States. Most countries had come against America in the recent decades because of their support for Israel, and the country had slowly become a modern day Sodom and Gomorrah. Crime rates were higher now than in any other place in the world; all the prisons that weren't full were still under new construction. With all of the issues at home and elsewhere, the U.S. government was moving to establish a new universal order under the authority of the United Nations. The churches had already lost their rights, and now everything else was about to change. Those with the authority knew that if the most countries merged with the United Nations, there would simply come to be one currency, one state, and one religion. They also knew that anyone who then expressed a belief outside of this New Union would inevitably be considered a national criminal.

Many Christians rebelled against America for even considering this grandiose affront to freedom. They knew that if this merger went into effect, Jesus Christ would be banned, and anyone confessing their faith in Him would be severely punished. Children over the age of 12 were to be considered adults under the proposed changes of the new government, so they too were fully susceptible to the new punishments of the adults. Tragically, the parents of those children who were not Christians were more protected than those whose parents were.

Brian and Sophia however were no longer aware of this struggle, and did not think it was possible for two people to be happier. For a month, they had no worries whatsoever, just happiness and peace. The girls' caretaker had the number to call if they needed to; but for one month, Brian and Sophia were in a world of their own. They did not look at television; they did not listen to the radio; they did not use a computer; and no phone calls came in or out. It was just Jesus and them.

But after the honeymoon, Brian and Sophia were anxious to get back home to their daughters. While on the plane, Brian kept wondering why he had been granted so much happiness and peace.

It seemed to Brian then that a voice said, "Enjoy it, while it lasts."

He turned to Sophia, "Did you hear that?"

Sophia took off her headphones, "Hear what?"

"Some voice just said, "enjoy it while it lasts."

"Oh Brian, the song that I'm listening to is called "Enjoy it while it lasts. Perhaps you heard the song?"

"No, I didn't hear anything like that; it was a voice that said it, almost in a whisper."

"Brian, I think the Lord is trying to tell us something."

"I think I agree," Brian said.

Brian was disturbed over some of the recent news he had heard while on the airplane back to the United States. Reportedly, North and South America had finally gone ahead and merged with the United Nations.

"Sophia, I'm afraid that things might be changing for us soon here in America"

"In what way Brian?"

"The countries are collecting, and soon it seems that we will no longer be given the free choice of what we want to believe in."

"Yes, Brian, unfortunately I know what you mean. Seven years ago I tried to ban all Christians from the country, and now I think it is actually going to happen."

"As bad as it's going to be, I'm more worried about Israel. The only reason that the rest of the world has left them alone this long is because the United States has always helped them to defend themselves. But even if we stop, I cannot see Israel accepting a one-world religion. For many years, the Jews were adamant in their belief that there is only one God. If they accept this new one world religion, they would be giving up everything they had ever fought for. Most of them would probably rather die" Brian and Sophia did not arrive in Fergus Falls until late that night.

For the peaceful years that followed, just the joy of having God in their lives together was happiness enough. However, to have the Lord and each other was more than they ever could have imagined. Brian had taken a good paying job working as a biologist for the government. Essentially, his job was to make sure diseases didn't become epidemics. Sophia had previously been working with an anti-religious group before her coma, but hadn't worked a day ever since. She'd been living off her savings and the money Brian brought home, which was more than enough to keep them comfortable. The two of them didn't have a care in the world. With three beautiful daughters and all the money they needed, things couldn't have been better.

Every day, Brian looked at Sophia's olive complexion, her black hair, and her dark brown eyes; those eyes were full of love and joy. Sophia looked at Brian's tall, lean, well-built body and couldn't help but smile. He had dark brown hair and an olive tint to him like hers. They looked so much alike that they could have sometimes passed as brother and sister. It was like a match made in heaven. On the weekends, they kissed and made love all day. Sometimes, they would just sit on the porch in the cool air to soak in each other's presence, looking longingly at one another for hours without saying one word. The weather was very amiable too. It was not too cold, yet not too hot, but somewhere well established in-between. All the while, God allowed them this happiness because of the turmoil that they had come through already, and the turmoil that was yet to come.

Chapter 32

As the world stirred, Satan came again and presented himself before the throne of God. The Lord spoke, "Why are you here?"

Satan replied, "You have put a hedge around Brian and Sophia for seven years now."

The Lord looked at Satan with a sad expression on his face, "It was their time to rest." Satan was angry because he wanted the Lord to show His emotions of hate as he was known to. Satan loved to make God upset.

He spoke to God in an angry tone: "It isn't a fair fight! I can't even tempt them?!"

The Lord looked at Satan with pity, and said, "It is true, their rest is up. They have seen my goodness in their lives, and will not fail me."

"We will see!" Satan laughed.

"Be gone now you fiend!" The Lord demanded with a loud thunder.

Immediately upon his disappearance, Satan called upon several hundreds of his demons. "Now, I want you to instigate trouble with the United States government against Brian and Sophia.

In the current state of things, North America had fallen under attack from multiple different countries. The weather there was also changing, and the U.S. was financially bankrupt because of the many wars, earthquakes, hurricanes, tornadoes, volcanoes, massive floods, and fires that had destroyed so many trees, occurring so frequently year after year. In very little time at all, the coastlines of most cities were no longer there anymore due to the irregularity of a water supply. There were problems with our atmosphere as well, as the greenhouse effect had evaporated most of the remaining fresh water; the air was polluted, and the deserts were increasing, with the ice caps melting rapidly. Because of this melting, many floods were also occurring. This is what caused the coastline of most cities to be destroyed. Many animals and birds had quickly become extinct because of the many fires in wooded areas. Many of the fish in the rivers, streams, lakes and oceans died because of the polluted waters. Insects were increasing because the many birds that ate them had died. Because the numbers of insects had increased, mankind tried to eliminate them with poisons. Unfortunately, the poisons that the government spread on the insects polluted not only the air and fresh waters, but caused many more diseases to spread as well. Many people died of diseases; the vaccines the doctors had used in the past did not work anymore.

Religion was one of the issues that was a concern to the New Union. Many disputes came about because of the different religions, so a vote was inevitably cast to have one religion. Jesus Christ was not accepted. They voted for one God for everyone, instead of a God that demanded sacrifice. Anyone teaching about Jesus Christ would thereafter be beheaded. Christians had lost their rights.

It was fall, and America had just merged with the New Union. The public schools were still free, but they did not pledge allegiance to the flag anymore. Brian and Sophia knew that trouble was in the air for people in old America. Everywhere in the world, the currency was changing, and the school children were noticing differences in their history classes. The teachers put more emphasis on the benefits of the unionization of the United Nations. Most countries had decided to come together under this New Union. They thought they needed to pool their resources together.

Freedom was taken away from most people, especially the Christians, and those who did not have the money to voice their opinions. The system that the New Union set up was to kill anyone teaching that this new government would one day be over-thrown. Therefor, the government came against all Christians who preached about the kingdom and Jesus Christ. The New Union did not like the idea of someone else taking over the government; they considered this behavior treason, and it was one of the reasons why people were beheaded. The people in charge felt as if the Christians were trying to cause a rebellion against the state by saying that Jesus Christ was the way to go. The New Union wanted to keep the peace with all religious groups, and the different nations that joined themselves to them. The government was also afraid that a civil war might be brought on by the confusion of the different religious teachings. Many religious groups did not see Jesus as the coming Messiah, and most people of the world did not see Jesus Christ as God. The world was in turmoil and needed answers, so the Christian faith became the scapegoat that the government chose to blame.

The world was in an economic disaster, and the New Union was looking for answers. The problem of overpopulation was still an issue even though many people had died from natural disasters. The world's political powers were looking for someone or something that was able to get the economy stable. All were desperate for answers and willing to take anyone's advice; it did not even matter if it was immoral.

The world found a man who was very handsome, and had no desire for women. Besides having powers to heal the sick and raise the dead, this man seemed to have the answers to the problems of the world. He was so cunning with his speech that the Jews believed he was from the lost tribe of Dan. Unofficially, they received him as their long awaited Messiah. The New Union was happy that he brought peace to Israel, even though it came as a result of a violation of the new religious laws. Nevertheless, this man became the Anti-Christ. He pretended to believe in some higher being to please the majority of the people that had faith in such things. In truth though, he didn't believe or bow to anyone but himself. Inevitably, he was against Christians because they would not accept anyone as the Savior but Jesus Christ.

Satan possessed this man by putting his own spirit to work in him. Essentially, Satan was in human flesh. He could do so much more in this world now that he had a position of power in it. After all, humankind had been given dominion over the earth. Even though Satan was called the god of this world, he was not physically present in it, and humans are influenced most by what they can see.

131

Because the man chosen by The New Union was so immoral, many people besides Christians came against his immorality. Jews, Muslims, Buddhists, Hindus, Atheists, Agnostics and other moral individuals started to agree that the behaviors of society were growing more and more evil. Money now carried absolute power and could literally buy the rich out of anything. Because so many groups cried out against the evil of children being sold for prostitution, the hierarchies of the world were in conflict with themselves.

The Anti- Christ thereby came up with a solution. He proposed that anyone who came against the government and its decisions was to be killed. In order to help society and the economy, he suggested that they rid it of the undesirables: anyone who was disabled, and was not able to make a difference to society would be put to sleep. Surprisingly, the plan was almost unanimously accepted by the New Union, even though many people cried out against such cruel behavior.

After he organized this new policy and the destruction of the Great Mosque, the Anti-Christ set himself up as god in the New Temple of Jerusalem. Finally seeing his true nature, the Jews in Israel rebelled against this man they had thought had come from the tribe of Dan, denouncing him as their messiah. However, as members of the New Union, all nations came against Israel. The Anti-Christ was able to influence the whole world; nevertheless, many people became Christians. In order to develop a solution to the world's hunger problems, this new leader persuaded many nations that they should only keep alive those who were healthy and faithful to the government. In order to prevent mass genocide, he told the world that these people could also be put in tight quarters in concentration camps. This action provoked the Christians as well as many other religious groups because they knew this was wrong.

Because the people who rebelled against this Anti-Christ were causing so much trouble, they were put thereby put in concentration camps all over the world; they were given very little food and sometimes not given any food for weeks. Millions starved to death in the first few months in these camps.

Many of the countries of the world were so corrupt that if a stranger came to a town or city, they were often abused, and sometimes even raped. Yet, those who had money were not charged with crimes no matter how inhuman they were; all they had to do was pay a fine. The New Union needed money, so they forgave anyone with money. It was almost impossible for the poor, elderly, disabled, and children to survive without someone to defend them; it was a world seemingly without hope. Social Security was stopped, even though many of the elderly had paid in when they had been working. The people in control were afraid, and did not know what to do, so the only solution was to get rid of the undesirables.

The government wanted to put the elderly, who were sick and unable to take care of themselves, to sleep. Most people in society did not come against these suggestions because the world had become desensitized to injustice. There were many runaways in the world; there were no charity churches for them to go to because the Christians were being persecuted for their faith.

Because many Christians, Jews, Muslims and other people who did not agree with the immoral behavior of society refused to take the mark of the beast, they lost their previous lives and properties. Anyone taking the mark of the beast was agreeing with the horrible immoral behaviors that this new organization stood for. Those who held on to their beliefs and were fortunate enough to evade the consecration camps were not able to buy and sell, and had to find other means of acquiring goods. Through the underground market, illegally operated by merchants with the mark, these outcasts were able to survive through trade. After all, business was business. In order to survive, many of the outcasts had to band together to live. Many Christians were able to persuade many Jews, Muslims and others who did not believe as the Christians believed that Jesus Christ was truly the Messiah.

The Lord spoke to some of the angels and told them that Brian's daughters and son-in-law would soon be killed.

"I want you to stand by Brian and Sophia at this time. Whisper in their ears the words of comfort that they will need.

The demons will be tormenting them. I want you to knock the demons out of the way every time they whisper doubt in Brian and Sophia's minds."

Chapter 33

At this point, Brian and Sophia had been married for seven years. They did not know anyone could still be so happy. Their oldest daughter Laquasha had met a man named Malik from the tribe of Levi. Born in Israel, he was a Rabbi who had become a Christian. Eventually, Malik and Laquasha were married. After they talked it over with Brian and Sophia, Malik then made armaments to move back to Israel to live. Brian and Sophia were heartbroken; therefore Brian decided that they would all move to Israel.

While living in Israel Malik had a zeal for the Lord, and Laquasha was caught up in the zeal too. Even in the face of the oppression of the New Union, their enthusiasm led them to the street corners, proclaiming the gospel of Jesus Christ and talking about the atrocities of the new government. Brian cautioned them about being too vocal in the face of the new laws, but neither his daughters nor his son-in-law would listen.

Brian's daughters and son-in-law knew what the law said about telling others that Jesus Christ would be coming back to set up a kingdom. Brian had cautioned them, but they had ignored the law of the land. They refused to stop testifying about the coming of the new government that Jesus Christ would rule. They were determined to win as many souls to Him before the second coming.

One day, Brian and Sophia were at home enjoying themselves, when the anointing of the Holy Spirit came upon Brian in a travailing prayer. Brian was weeping on the floor for three hours speaking in tongues. The Holy Spirit was praying in Brian because the Lord knew what he was about to face. Sophia did not do anything but pray in silence. Three days after Brian prayed in such an emotional way, he received a phone call. Brian's daughters and son-in-law had been arrested. Brian and Sophia rushed down to the jail, but there was no bail. The court date was already set for the next day, and the judge showed no mercy. The penalty was death to anyone saying Jesus Christ was the only hope for Salvation.

Even though Ryan was paralyzed in the hospital, he still had great power, and had been able to influence those in high positions in the New Union by possessing one of its leaders. Ryan then spoke through the man's body and suggested that if anyone had the audacity to speak out in public about Jesus Christ, he or she should be beheaded without a trial. Taking this action against Christians put fear in the people and kept them from rebelling. Not only were Brian's children about to be killed, but when this law went into effect, were millions of Christians beheaded for breaking it.

Everything happened so fast: the jail, the court, and the sentence. Around noon the next day, Brian's daughters and son-in-law were beheaded. Brian and Sophia were in shock: they still did not believe that their children could have been beheaded. Sophia was worried because it seemed to her that Brian was losing his hold on reality. Sophia knew Brian was still in shock; he did not cry enough for her.

"Lord!" Sophia prayed, "What can I do? Brian's heart is not here. He has not accepted the fact that the children are gone."

The Lord whispered to Sophia, "Just let him be; I will bring him around." Sophia wanted to feel all of Brian's pain, and soon she began to. The demons tormented Brian and Sophia's minds after the death of their children.

The Lord spoke to thousands of his angles, "I want you to fight for Brian and Sophia. They are all torn up inside from the death of their children."

A demon whispered in Brian's ear, "God doesn't love you. If he loved you, he would have protected your daughters and son-in-law." Brian felt an agony that no physical pain could match. Brian started to cry non-stop. Sophia remembered what the Lord said to her, to let him be.

An angel spoke in Brian's ear, "The Lord wishes you good and not evil." In response, a demon tried to whisper in Brian's ear again. The angel knocked the demon a half mile away.

136

This demon then asked ten other demons to help him destroy Brian while he was still hurting. When the demon came back, ten other angels were waiting there. In an instant, Fear gripped the demons, so they ran. The demons came back with 500 demons. While the ten angels fought some of the demons, the other demons tormented Brian's mind. They continued to say over and over, "God didn't care about your feelings; he could have saved your daughters." Against their expectations, the angels gave each demon a terrible beating. The horde never came back to torment Brian again.

Meanwhile Sophia was watching Brian while he was crying on the floor. He was rolling back and forth on the soft carpet in their apartment. Somewhere deep inside, Brian knew in himself that the Lord would not put more on him then he could bear. Sophia started to call out to the Lord to please help Brian.

Finally, the Lord himself appeared to Brian and Sophia. There was a very bright presence in the room. It was dark outside and the light almost blinded their eyes. The Lord dimmed his radiance and took on the form of Jesus Christ. The Lord opened Brian and Sophia's eyes with the brightness of Himself. It was still very bright in the room. The two of them saw not only the Lord, but ten angels standing very tall next to Him. After that, God helped Brian get to his feet, and He dried Brian's tears with a handkerchief. The Lord then embraced Brain, and He also embraced Sophia in His arms. Brian was overwhelmed because of the brightness around him. He looked into the Lord's face; there was so much love in the Lord's eyes for Brian and Sophia. Brian and Sophia did not know that Sophia had conceived the day before they received the news of their children's arrest.

The Lord said to the angels, "Once they find out the news about the baby, they will be comforted. Satan and his demons will try to make Sophia lose the child. I want all of you to fight against the demons so they won't hurt Sophia's baby; I want you to comfort Brian and Sophia when the demons torment their minds over the loss of their children; and I want you to let them know that because their children were killed, many more souls would be won. Every time someone hears their story, it is going to glorify Me. Once Brian and Sophia realize their children won more souls in death than in life, they will see the value in the instance."

When Brian and Sophia learned how their children had won thousands of souls to Jesus Christ on the one night they had been in prison, their sorrow was at last satiated with an overwhelming joy. Those individuals, who had rebelled when they'd heard about the injustices of the world, rebelled against the system and received Christ, even thought they knew it would mean certain death.

Chapter 34

Every time someone was now beheaded for the testimony of Jesus Christ and the blood of the lamb, it was put in a special paper in that town or county. The New Union wanted to discouraged anyone from believing what the Christians had to say. When Susan heard that her daughters were all killed, she wept endlessly. For years, Susan had been trying to find Brian. But Brian did not know how to get in touch with Susan after she had left him. He never got any information from Susan, and she had never told him where her father or brothers lived. The newspaper at last revealed the location of where Brian lived, so Susan rushed out the next day to find Brian. She knew he might run to a new location after his children had been beheaded, and it turned out that she was right because the government was looking for him; everyone in his family who was found was beheaded as well, simply on the principle of associating with Christians.

Susan, however, was able to make it to the burial of the girls. When she saw Brian and a stranger hanging back at the funeral to avoid calling attention, she was overjoyed to see him again. After all of the appropriate introductions, the three of them had a profound heart-to-heart; Susan at last told Brian everything that had happened to her while she was in the marriage with him for ten Years. She told Brian how Pastor Ryan had raped her, and how their youngest daughter was the product of that forced experience. Susan told Brian that she had been afraid to tell him what was going on, because Ryan went through the walls. Susan also mentioned to Brian that after Pastor Ryan rape her, several weeks later; he'd brought five more pastors with him to rape her. She knew now that Satan's plan had been to drive her away from Brian. It had worked because Susan was so unstable already from having been raped when she was only ten. This incident with her pastor had brought all the horrible memories back.

Susan told Brian that before she was diagnosed with AIDS, she had worked at a hospital, and met Ryan dying in his bed. There was no medication they could find to relieve him of his pain. Susan also told him how Ryan had pleaded with her to forgive him.

He'd kept saying, "I am going to hell; please forgive me. I see now everything that I did to you and the others; the pain, the torment, the genocide. I can't die, but I can't live with myself over this either."

Susan, at this time, had not yet given herself to Jesus Christ; "Why don't you believe what you preach?" Susan said. "I believe Jesus will forgive you; even though I couldn't prove you allowed these ministers to come through walls, I felt sadness for you then. I knew you were a coward to pick on a woman with issues. I now know in my heart that Satan was trying to make me hate God though, and not you. So I forgive you now, as I have come to realize that I don't hate God; in fact, I am blessed. I didn't realize evil people like you existed before. Therefore, I had always told myself that it was just me. But you made me believe in me, and that I wasn't such a terrible person. So I forgive you, and those who once did me wrong."

Ryan started to cry; he grabbed her hand while tears fell from his face.

"I believe God has forgiven me Susan, but I had to see you before I died." That same day Ryan died, and Susan gave her heart to Jesus Christ.

Susan continued to explain her story to Brian: "I knew I couldn't continue to live with you Brian, after being raped by Ryan and the five pastors in the spirit world. So I left. You were a good husband and a good father, so I left the girls with you. I knew I couldn't teach them to love like you could. Afterwards, I prayed to God one day allow me the chance to tell you I'm sorry. As I was trying to convince Ryan that Jesus Christ loves him, I realized he loves me too. So Ryan and I both received Christ on the same day. The Lord was pacified and allowed Ryan to die in peace after he received him as his Lord and Savior. Ryan died five minutes after he thanked me for forgiving him and leading him to Jesus Christ the Savior; but I still felt a peace that I have never felt before after I received Christ in my life."

After Susan told Brian what happened to her when she left him, she finally asked Brian to forgive her. "I could not stay with you before because I did not know what to do with my messed up emotions, and I could not handle everything that was happening to me. Most of all, I did not know how to tell you that our younger daughter Diane was not yours, but Ryan's."

Susan turned to Sophia, "You have the best man any woman could dare to hope for." Tears ran down Susan's cheek as she spoke. Sophia put her arms around Susan and hugged her for a few minutes while they cried together. When they were finished, Brian hugged her and cried with her about their children who had been beheaded. As Brian was hugging Susan, she cried in a loud voice, "Oh, how I wanted to see my daughters again, to ask for their forgiveness for leaving them."

Brian responded in tears, "They forgave you the very night you left." And Susan wept with both joy and sorrow

Three days later, Susan died of complications from her AIDS. Brian was so overwhelmed with everything Susan had told him and what had been happening lately, he could barely process it all. Fortunately, these events brought Brian and Sophia out of the shock that their son-in-law and three daughters had just been buried. After Brian and Sophia buried Susan, they knew that they had to run to the mountains.

After arriving at Mount Kilimanjaro, Brian started thinking about the last time he had been in heaven. The Lord had known Satan had the right to accuse the five pastors who stood before Him; they had raped Susan; they had no fear of God, and they would abuse the implications of forgiveness in His Word. Brian had asked Him, "Who are they, Lord?" The Lord spoke in a soft voice, "Brian, you're not ready for that now." Brian accepted His judgment, and did not ask any more questions. He did not know it was his first pastor, Ryan, and his second wife, Kelsey, as well as many of the other pastors in that organization, who were being accused by Satan.

The Lord felt a strong anger within Himself: *How many times did I plead with them to repent and turn from their evil ways? All Ryan and Kelsey did with these pastors was to laugh at me for forgiving them of their sins. They abused my sheep, and abused the gifts that I allowed them for satisfying their own lust. It would not hurt me so much if they had just sinned against me, but they looked for the weakest saints, who were already hurting, and abused them as if it were a sport.*

The Lord was also thinking about Brian while Satan was accusing the five pastors. The Lord was about to weep when He thought about how innocent Brian was while he sat at the foot of His throne.

Two days after their children were buried Sophia learned that she was pregnant. When she told Brian, he felt as though his heart would explode into tears

"Brian? You're not happy about having another child?" Sophia questioned meekly.

"That's not the reason I'm crying love; I'm crying because I never expected such a gift in the times we live in." Brian took Sophia in his arms and drew her in for a kiss. "Sophia, the Lord knows how much we can bear."

In that moment, a demon whispered in Brian ear, "It is starting all over again; your life is going to be a living hell. Next, they will kill Sophia and the baby to be, and your faith will be the undoing of everything you love. Stop this foolishness; just stop telling people that Jesus saves. You did enough for Him.

Sophia was also tormented by the forces of darkness: "If Brian is killed, what would you do? You can't make it by yourself. Even if the baby is born, the Lord is probably going to allow it to die too. He is only thinking about Himself. He just wants to boast about how much you love Him through your suffering."

"But think on God's word," the angels said to Sophia.

And Sophia spoke, "The Lord wishes me good and not evil, so be gone you evil spirit." But the demons just laughed at Sophia.

So the angels told Brian to sing, and his voice was like a river that burst the dam: "I will trust in the Lord until I die." Soon, Sophia too joined in on the song, and in the wake of their music the demons disappeared.

The Lord then told the angels, "I want Brian and Sophia to have some peace for the next two years."

Chapter 35

After Sophia came to Jesus and came out of the coma, she had begun to pray for her family. After the New Union formed, her parents finally called her because they were afraid of what was happening to America. They felt that some things were not right; mostly, they did not want to take the mark of the beast. Sophia convinced them to listen to the Lord's message, and after much prayer, Sophia's parents believed and received Christ into their lives. Her parents were then able to convince Walter that Christ was the one and only savior. Because Sophia's parents and cousin had high positions in society but refused to take the mark of the New Union, they were beheaded.

As a result of Brian's praying for his family and step-father for many years, they all eventually came to Christ, and refused to take the mark of the New Union. Therefore, they were all put in a concentration camp. Meanwhile, Brian and Sophia did not witness much while Sophia was with child. They moved up into the mountains with many other Christians. People dug holes in the ground for shelter, and some lived in caves. They had all the conveniences a person might need in a household. Many of the people who lived on the mountains were electricians, carpenters, teachers, doctors, and had all the skills that were needed in an underground society.

As the world continued down its path, Satan knew he did not have much time to win more souls to himself. Satan did not want any souls left when Jesus Christ came back to set up His government on the earth. Satan's whole purpose was to kill, steal, and destroy all that the Lord had made that would give Him pleasure and glory. Satan had to call many meetings against Christians with his demons, especially against Brian and Sophia. Satan hated the two of them because they always praised the Lord no matter what they suffered. This made Satan unwaveringly frustrated. He just could not accept that someone could love God so unconditionally. Satan knew that this is what he should have done before he sinned against the Lord; Satan knew he had lost the battle, but he wanted to destroy as many souls' as he could. Sometimes, while Satan was looking at Brian and Sophia's happiness, he wished he too could have such happiness. He knew his judgment was already set by God. Deep down, Satan did not know why he was so determined to fight against God. He thought back to when he was the Lord's anointed and when he had covered the throne of God. He felt the Lord's love so strongly for him then. How he wished he could go back to that very second just to bathe in the love of God again.

But Satan never did understand the concept of love. Now he realized he should not have questioned God. He remembered seeing Jesus Christ in hell some time later, taking the keys of death and hell from him. Satan remembered how defeated he had felt. He knew he had lost the battle then. He had not known he was crucifying the Lord of glory. Satan did not know love was that strong. He almost dropped on his knees in hell but his pride would not let him. He remembered not knowing what to do next.

After the Christians started to die for their faith, Satin decided to become a part of their Christian church by allowing the Roman Empire to embrace Christianity. He remembered being furious with many Christians who would always stand for what was right. Satan wanted to show God that no one would serve Him, and through the years, the Christians had proven that they would love the Lord no matter what they suffered.

"Oh, why don't they just curse God and die? If everyone would have turned against God then I would not be so afraid." Now, Satan was trembling because he knew Jesus Christ would come back very soon, and his time would then be up.

Chapter 36

Brian and Sophia now lived high in the Kilimanjaro Mountains. Many of the Christians lived in a cave in the mountain side, eating whatever they could find in the mountains. One of the main dishes was grasshoppers. Occasionally, the Lord sent His angels to speak to the birds and animals to bring food to the Christians. With his divine hand he would lead deer, rabbits, goats, and grasshoppers to come to this mountain. Some of the Christians were even skilled enough to grow gardens, which God made to grow potatoes, cabbage, collard greens, corn, and beets. Sometimes, flocks of birds would drop bags of food that they could not grow in their gardens. In one instance, a flock of birds even dropped gallons of frozen ice cream for the people to enjoy; there was every flavor that the mind could imagine. Another time, a flock of birds dropped pounds of hot, baked bread – new age manna from the heavens.

The Mountains were cool and beautiful; there was a waterfall only a half-an-hour's walk from where Brian and Sophia lived. The seclusion was practically impenetrable, as it was very hard to get up to where they were in the mountains; even planes and helicopters had a hard time getting anywhere near where the refugees were staying. Eventually though, rumors spread to the surrounding country of a place of escape in the African mountains; and after a time, Brian and Sophia's hiding place was inevitably discovered. A warlock name Clarriko had pretended he was a Christian, and infiltrated their camp for a few weeks before disappearing from the community. He informed the New Union where the Christians were gathering, and helped to organize a strike to purify the countryside. During the attack, many planes and helicopters tried to land in the mountains. Some of the Christians' homes were deep in the earth, while others lived in caves; so it would take a large force to sweep them all out. As some of the aircraft began to land, the Christians cried out to the Lord for help.

Almost instantly, the winds of the mountain spiked between 70 and 160 miles an hour. Already flying in a thin atmosphere, the planes and helicopters were dashed against the mountains. Everyone in them was killed. The Christians were miraculously saved, and the New Union never again came against the Christians on that front.

Sophia was two months with child when the authorities had tried to capture them, and she cried out with joy after God's deliverance. Brian hugged Sophia with a tremendous bear hug.

"We don't have to worry about anyone bothering us up here anymore. I feel it in my spirit."

Sophia smiled, "I feel it too, like the Lord is sheltering us in the clouds of this sanctuary."

Then the two of them began to sing hymns and praises to the Lord. Other Christians soon joined in the singing, and the celebration grew into a realized festival of faith. Someone had a portable piano, and even the angels smiled and joined in the singing. The Lord was very pleased. They worshipped Him for hours, until the moon and stars lit up the heavens. The Christians on the mountain knew now that they would be taken care of until Jesus Christ returned, and they rejoiced in the mercy and love of God.

Even though these people had to work hard for their lives, it was exciting because it made them think of how people in the past had lived. Everyone on the mountain was well organized, with each person using their skills to benefit the whole of the community. The doctors, teachers, lawyers and laymen all helped to provide food and shelter for the community. Some of the Christians would do the hunting, while others did the fishing in the nearby stream, and still others would do the gardening before the cooler weather came. Others would try and devise new ways to keep everyone warm in the wettest and coldest months, which only ranged from a 64 degree low to a 92 degree high. Stories would be told of the many miracles the Lord had done; and He gave wisdom to each person on how to survive by encouraging the knowledge the teachers, doctors, and lawyers were able to teach.

As the months passed, Sophia grew to seven months with child; Brian did not think a woman could be so beautiful.

When she fussed about her looks, he told her, "Sophia, there is no beauty compared to you with our child." Always, she would blush, and they grew closer and closer together. The two of them had never known that love making could bring such joy and happiness. The excitement was waking up in the morning to see the smile on each other's' faces. Even when Sophia had nearly carried the baby to term, Brian still found her beautiful to look at. It was now only two weeks before Sophia's baby would be born.

On one of these nights, Brian was home alone, while some of the ladies on the mountain were having an all-night baby shower before Sophia's baby was born.

A demon spoke to Brian in his solitude, "Sophia and the baby will die while Sophia gives birth. God wants to test your faith with their death." Brian expression was calm. "You are a liar; God told me to trust him, and I know He won't give me more than I can bear." And the demon left, as they often did, because he could not upset Brian's faith.

When at last it came to the night Sophia was to give birth, the pain became very intense for Sophia. Many times, she passed into a coma. But Brian, ever vigilant, kept praying her out of them. It was hard for the baby to be born in this natural setting; when Sophia went into a coma, she could not continue to push the baby out. On the mountain, the Christians did not have all of the conveniences of modern medicine, so Brian and others who were helping with the birth were afraid the baby might die in the womb.

As their efforts grew tense, Brian spoke to God, "Lord, if you want this baby to be born, then let nothing stand in its way." In a fury none of them could see, Brian and Sophia's angels fought against the demons that were trying to kill her and the baby. But the demons ran when their defeat became eminent. Then at last, their son was born.

Brian and Sophia's baby boy was named Barry; that he might one day held spearhead God's revolution. The happiness they felt was beyond all sense of experience; there was no word to express their happiness. Brian and Sophia had many tears of joy because Barry was born from their beautiful love, and the love of God. They could not thank the Lord enough for giving them so much happiness. Even though their life was still spent in hiding, they woke up every morning with newfound happiness. Barry looked just like Brian.

Now that their son was born, the Lord wanted Brian and Sophia to transport their bodies to different places in the world. The Lord promised Brian and Sophia that he would always provide a way of escape for them and their son. Barry was only three months when the Lord spoke to them about their transporting missions. He told them He needed them to encourage the Christians who were in concentration camps and the souls who were about to be beheaded. God also wanted them to win more souls to Him, ensuring Brian and Sophia that He was coming back to set up his new kingdom very soon.

He said, "I want you to tell everyone you meet that I will soon reclaim my place as the ruler of this world. Remind them of why I died, that they might be worthy to stand by my side."

Chapter 37

Over the next few weeks, Brian and Sophia learned to transport their whole bodies to someplace else and transport them back home safely. The whole time, they wondered how the Lord would transport their bodies with the newborn baby Barry. An even bigger question in their minds was why God wanted Barry to go with them in the first place.

As Sophia and Brian were discussing the matter amongst themselves, the Lord joined in on their conversation and asked, "Is there anything too hard for Me?"

"No, Lord," Brian and Sophia laughed as one, instantly relieved by His words. That night the Lord spoke to Brian and Sophia again. He told them to transport their bodies and their son to Israel before the start of the new day. So just before midnight, Brian, Sophia, and Barry sat together and held hands. They closed their eyes and thought about Jerusalem. Astonishingly, even at the age of three months, Barry understood and followed what his parents did.

Brian and Sophia called out together, "Take us, Lord, to the place you want us to go." In their minds, they felt themselves spinning with such a speed until they were caught up in the air. They no longer experienced the world through their five senses. It seemed like only moments before they found themselves sitting on the outskirts of Jerusalem. They opened their eyes to be greeted by open meadow. There were two people standing there looking at them when their bodies appeared in the concentration camp. Both figures nearly flew away with the surprise on their faces. Sophia was holding the baby, and Brian was holding both of them; they found themselves in a valley in Israel with people who were about to be beheaded the next day. There were 16 men and 13 women. A few children were there too. Some of them were Christians, and some were people who opposed the New Union for its cruelty to mankind. Some people were there only because they were disabled. But the fences were too high to climb for anyone. Even if they tried to climb the fence, they would have been electrocuted or shot. The Christians actually looked fairly healthy, but many of the others were wasting away from hunger. After they overcame their astonishment, the Christians told Brian and Sophia that they had prayed for the Lord to send his messenger to them before they were beheaded. They had praised the Lord when he had sent them food and answered their prayers. The Christians had always shared with the other prisoners, and a few had already turned their souls to Christ. Brian spoke and told them the good news; how God sent His Son in the flesh so that he could shed His blood for the sins of the world; and how God wanted their love. If by faith they believed, the righteousness of His Son Jesus Christ would be spread to them, and the Lord would see that they had been cleansed. If they received this good news and repented of their sins, the Lord would welcome them to Himself.

Brian also told them the good news of the kingdom of God, and that if they believed these things, they would reign with Jesus Christ in the second coming. Even though some of these captives had seen many miracles, they did not want to believe that Brian, Sophia, and Barry had appeared from nowhere. Some doubted.

They said things like, "This is not real," and "this is just an illusion."

Sophia asked the man who was blind, "Do you believe we are an illusion?"

The blind man said, "I can't see you, but I hear and feel your presence."

Sophia nodded and relied, "Do you believe that Jesus died for your sins and that He rose again on the third day to justify you?"

"Yes, I believe!" the blind man said with hope in his voice. Brian and Sophia asked together, "Do you believe Jesus' back was beaten so that you could be healed?"

"Yes!" the blind man said with tears running down his eyes. Brian and Sophia put their hands on the man's eyes and watched as they were opened. Witnessing this, the Christians and newfound believers raised their voices and praised the Lord in song.   In such a way, The Lord used Brian and Sophia not only to encourage the Christians, but anyone who believed in His righteousness, goodness, mercy and justice. Despite that some in the camp were not sure what to believe, they all joined in singing with the Christians, "Now I know my Redeemer lives."   The more they sang about the redeemer, the more everyone wanted to believe in this Jesus Christ as their savior. They all knew that by noon tomorrow they would be killed. Still, many that were not Christians gave their lives to God that night by receiving Jesus Christ into their hearts.

There were still some of them that doubted though.

One Atheist said, "If this is all true, why doesn't the Lord get us out of this prison?" Of course, the Atheist didn't realize what he had said. He hadn't said, "Why doesn't your God get us out of this prison," but rather acknowledged the fact of the Lord presence.

Brian said, "I don't have all the answers. All I know is that the Lord transported our bodies here to bring you the good news of salvation, and to tell you about how He will set up His kingdom when he comes back. Won't you receive Jesus Christ into your life?"

Everyone said, "Yes!" Many who said this would not have given their lives to God or believed that Jesus Christ is the Messiah if they had not been backed into a corner. But God forgave them anyway. Brian, Sophia and everyone started to sing, "He lives, and I know my Jesus lives." As everyone was singing, many people were healed. The Lord filled everyone with His spirit and they all spoke in tongues as the spirit gave them utterance. Brian and Sophia kissed everyone before they left, though everybody wanted to hold the baby Barry. The children were happy to hear that some day they would see Barry again in that new kingdom. Then Brian, Sophia, and Barry held on to each other, and found themselves back home on their mountain.

When their two years of peace had passed, Satan was furious because Brian and Sophia were winning so many souls to Christ. Satan was also upset because everywhere Brian and Sophia went they would tell about a better government that was coming soon, and Jesus Christ would be ruling in this new kingdom.

Satan spoke to the Lord, "You said that Brian and Sophia would only have two years of rest."

The Lord replied, "Yes."

"Their time is up," Satan smirked.

Before Barry turned two, the Lord had only led Brian and Sophia to places where people were able to speak their native language, as well as English. Before the Lord sent Brian and Sophia to a place that didn't speak English, He had to wait until their son Barry turned two years old. The Lord wanted to perform a miracle for those who were about to be beheaded the next day at noon. The miracle He chose was to allow Barry to translate his parents' words into any language. If those in the concentration camps all over the world didn't believe anything they heard or saw up to this point, they were convinced after hearing Barry translate the good news of Jesus Christ. Many times Brian, Sophia and Barry would travel all over the world, and Barry would interpret for them in this way.

As it would happen, Satan witnessed this miracle, and called a demon to attack Barry's voice. But the Lord called His angels to protect Barry. A demon tried to take Barry's voice away with a terrible cold. The cold was so bad that Barry could not speak because the coughing had made his throat sore. Brian and Sophia prayed for Barry to be healed by the beating Jesus took on his back. An angel fought the demon that was attacking Barry's throat. Satan was enraged because the Lord would not let him harm Brian, Sophia or Barry.

Sometimes Brian, Sophia, and Barry would meet other Christians who were able to transport their bodies, and they would take time out for a few minutes to encourage each other in the Lord. Sometimes the guards would see Brian, Sophia and Barry: they would not report them, but would talk to them and ask if they had a chance with Jesus Christ since they had taken the mark. Brian would tell them, "The Lord's mercy endures forever. Just tell the Lord you're sorry. He is the Judge."

One day while Brian and Sophia were relaxing in their cave, Barry wondered off to the nearby pond. Although Barry was three years old, he had the intelligence of a ten year old, even though his emotions were still that of a three year old. As Barry was sitting by a pond in the mountains, he heard an audible voice speaking to him. The voice said to Barry, "Don't you ever wonder what it is like to be on the other side, away from this mountain?" Barry spoke, "No." Even at the age of three, Barry was surprised that he would even doubt the Lord for a second. He had seen the Lord's goodness since he could remember. Another audible voice spoke to Barry, "Go tell your parents what just happened to you." Barry got up and said, "Okay!"

After Barry told his parents what happened, Brian and Sophia asked Barry what he thought about Jesus Christ. "He's my friend and Savior." Sophia asked Barry, "How do you know He's your Savior?"

"Because Jesus told me He is my savior." Barry smiled as he hugged his mom. Brian asked Barry, "When did Jesus tell you He was your Savior?"

"When I went to heaven," Barry said in a surprised voice. "Dad, don't you and mom go to heaven?"

Brian looked at Barry with a smile and asked him, "When did you go to heaven?

Barry laughed and said, "Dad, every night when I go to bed." Brian and Sophia looked at each other and praised the Lord for his goodness. They both put their arms around Barry and kissed him.

They said, "You go to heaven as much as you want."

When Barry was four years old, the Lord told Brian, Sophia, and Barry to transport their bodies to Singapore, to a playground where Christian children were playing. Their parents had been beheaded for their faith. The children did not speak the language that Brian and Sophia spoke, but Barry was able to talk them about Jesus. Children like these who were under the age of 12 were not allowed to take the mark of the beast.

One child said to Barry, "I want that Jesus you are talking about."

154

So Barry laid hands on the five year old and said, "Receive the Holy Ghost." The little boy fell back on the ground and started speaking in English, the language Brian and Sophia understood. He was saying, "I am pleased; I am pleased. I will be coming back soon, very soon; hold fast to your faith and be of good cheer." Together they all praised the Lord.

There were fifteen children in the playground when the little boy spoke in tongues. Their ages ranged from three years old to eleven. After witnessing this miracle, all of them wanted this Jesus. Brian, Sophia, and Barry laid hands on them and they all started speaking in tongues. They all were glorifying the Lord in English. Some adults saw what was happening to the children and called the authorities. Many police came out to arrest Brian and Sophia. Brian touched Sophia and Barry and just by thinking where they wanted to be, they vanished from sight. Brian, Sophia, and Barry instantly found themselves back home.

Barry said, "Mom I am tired."

Brian and Sophia agreed, "So are we." So they all had a peaceful sleep that night.

When Brian, Sophia, and Barry woke up the next morning, not only were the birds singing, but there was also a host of angles that had joined in. As far as they could see, there were angels in the sky. They all were dressed in long white robes. Many of the Christians that lived high up in the mountains came outside to see the angels sing such beautiful music that they had never heard before. The angels sang for three hours and then they were gone. Everyone praised God with joy, and danced for the Lord because of His mighty acts.

One night when Barry went to sleep, the Lord was excited because Barry always made Him laugh. The angels were also glad to see Barry because they loved to hear the Lord laugh. When God laughed, all of heaven felt His joy and happiness. Barry was five year old when these events happened in heaven. On another occasion, when Barry went to sleep and opened his eyes, he was in a garden. Jesus was sitting on a bench made of marble, white as snow.

"Well, My sunshine has arrived." The Lord smiled with happiness when He saw Barry. Barry smiled at the Lord as if He was an old friend. Barry sat on the bench next to the Lord.

"How did you become Jesus?" Barry asked the Lord.

"Barry, you wouldn't understand even if I tried to tell you," The Lord smiled.

"Lord, you could make my mind to understand if you really tried." Barry looked at the Lord with a serious stare.

The Lord laughed, "I can't argue with that." The Lord said. "Okay Barry, here goes; whatever you see is Me."

"That's no answer Lord, how did everything get here, including You?" The Lord laughed, and laughed. "Jesus, why are you laughing?" Barry said with tears starting to come to his eyes.

Jesus picked Barry up and said, "Because you are so funny. Barry, you want to know how I got here? Just think of it like this, I was here, and no one else was." The Lord was trying not to laugh. "Jesus, that is not telling me how you got here," Barry insisted. The Lord looked at Barry with an expression of wonder. "Only five years old and you want to know my secret. I tell you what I'm going to do. Words can never explain how I got here. Therefore, I'm going to put my fingers on your temples on both side of your head; my thoughts will go into your mind and then you will see how I got here."

When the Lord did this, Barry screamed, "Wow, wow, wow!" The Lord laughed so hard he wanted to just hug Barry.

"Now you know." The Lord hugged Barry and kissed him on his forehead.

When Barry woke up the next morning, Brian and Sophia noticed there was something different about Barry. Sophia asked him, "Honey, is everything alright?"

"Yes, Mom." Barry's mind was somewhere else as he spoke.

Brian said, "It looked like you were some place off in space."

"No Dad, I'm here. Brian gave Barry a warm hug.

"You know daddy and mommy love you. Any time you want to talk we are here for you." Brian said. Sophia hugged

156

Barry and gave him a kiss on his forehead. Barry smiled, and went to play with his toys.

Ever since the New Union killed millions of Christians at one time, it had gotten dark at noon. This had been going on for seven years now. Barry too was now seven years old. Often it was so dark people had to put their hand in front of them when they walked. The Christians were weary and crying out to the Lord to come and set up his kingdom. Brian and Sophia had seen so many of them die. Meanwhile, the majority of Jews from all over the world had turned their lives over to Jesus Christ and won many souls to God. They not only witnessed for Jesus Christ but also wailed with tears for the Messiah to come and set up His kingdom. Many knew that it would be Jesus Christ.

While all this excitement was going on with the Jews, Brian and Sophia were aware that when Barry turned 12, he could be caught and be beheaded. They both were sad when they thought that they might one day lose Barry. Barry brought so much joy and happiness to their lives. Brian and Sophia both agreed that if the Lord willed it, then they must let it be.

Brian and Sophia were so tired of seeing so many people killed every day, they just wanted to go home with the Lord. Barry had wanted to stay in heaven the last time he went. The Lord had told Barry he could stay, but his parents would be so sad if he died. So Barry had decided to come back on the earth to be with his parents. The Lord told Brian, Sophia, and Barry then that He was waiting for more souls to accept him, and as soon as the cup of iniquity was full, he will come back.

The Lord showed himself to Brian, Sophia, and Barry to encourage them. Sophia started to cry because so much was happening in the world, and yet she was privileged not only to have fellowship with the Lord, but also to see Him and touch Him. The Lord said, "Don't cry; I would never let something happen to you if it wasn't in my perfect plan."

Brian said, "Lord, I am crying because You are holding me in your arms. I don't know why Sophia is crying, but that's why I am."

Sophia started to smile and say, "I am crying now because You are holding me too tight Lord." Jesus smiled.

Barry said, "Jesus, where is my hug!" The Lord looked at Barry and said, "Sunshine you know there is always room in my arms for you." Barry ran to the Lord and leapt into His arms.

After everyone stopped laughing, the Lord had a sad look on his face.

He looked at Brian and Sophia and said, "There are still many souls in concentration camps all over this world I want you to win to me."

The next day, the Lord moved upon Brian, Sophia and Barry to transport their bodies to a concentration camp, which was in the former United Arab Emirates. Before they came through the walls, many Muslims were arguing with the Christians about the one God, Allah. One particular Muslim was an Agnostic, but because he had seen so many miracles while in the concentration camp, the Christians persuaded him that Jesus Christ was the Messiah. His brother was furious that he was converted to Christianity.

"You have no right to push your religion on my brother when he's not sure what to believe."

One Christian man spoke up, "We're not making anyone receive Jesus Christ, we are just telling what we experience with Him, and why the animals are coming through the holes in the walls and bringing us fresh food and water. It is a miracle, not only do the little animals bring us canned goods but can openers too, not even to mention that the bottles of water are sealed. This is why your brother has received Jesus Christ as his savior."

The Muslim man said, "It is not Jesus Christ that is doing these miracles but Allah. There are 60% Muslims in this concentration camp, and Allah is rewarding us because we took a stand against children being sold as sex slaves." Just then everyone saw three people come through the walls. Even the Christians were surprised.

Brian spoke, "The Lord loves you and wants you to believe that Jesus Christ paid the price that you might come boldly to God and asks for forgiveness for your sins." No one understood what he was saying. Then Barry, now seven years old, spoke in perfect Arabic and interpreted everything Brian said. Some of the people started crying. Many who were not sure what to believe received the message that Jesus Christ was indeed the savior of the world. Everyone knew that by noon the next day they would be beheaded, some for the testimony of Jesus Christ, and some because they rebelled against the New Union. Before Brian, Sophia and Barry went through the walls, everyone was crying because they did not think any God would love them this much.

After Brian, Sophia and Barry left the former United Arab Emirates, the Lord moved upon them to be transported to the former United States of America. The concentration camp was in Atlanta, Georgia, and 95% of the prisoners were Christians, while the other 5% were free thinkers. Even though the Christians had seen many miracles of the Lord sending the underground animals to bring fresh food and water, the Christians could not help but praise the Lord. Nevertheless, their bodies were tired after being in the concentration camp for four years. The Christians wanted the Lord to come back, so they travailed with loud tears of passion asking the Lord to come back and set up His kingdom. The 5%who were not Christians rejoice with them because they could not deny the goodness of the Lord. The Lord knew the Christians needed to be encouraged so He sent His trio to comfort them before they were beheaded. It was very hard for anyone to deny this last miracle of three people coming through the wall. So when Brian spoke, it was easy for all to accept Jesus Christ as their Lord and savior.

Before Brian, Sophia and Barry went on their next assignment, the Lord told them to rest for three days. Sometimes the Lord would move upon them to make three trips in one day. When they transported their bodies to different countries, the Lord allowed them to meet others who were performing His works so that they could encourage each other. The Lord only allowed up to three trips a day because it was too much for the body to transport more than three times.

After resting for three days, the Lord spoke to them around midnight, "I want the three of you to transport your bodies to India." The Lord spoke with great concern.

Barry spoke, yawning in a whisper, "Lord, I am sleepy." The Lord said, "I need you Barry to interpret for me." "O.K. Jesus, Barry said, rubbing his eyes.

Meanwhile, the New Union having a hard time with Hindus in India. They believed that if they did wrong in this life by killing anyone who was unable to defend themselves, they would have to answer to what they had done in their next lives. Therefore, many Hindus refused to take the mark and accept the atrocities the New Union proposed. There were some Christians who were put in the same concentration camps with the Hindus. This camp was outside, the Hindus had seen the birds bring fresh food and drink, but they were not convinced that Jesus Christ was responsible for this. They felt that the birds saw them starving in this camp, and were moved to bring food. The Christians tried to persuade them that God was showing his mercy and wanted all to come to repentance and receive Jesus Christ as Lord and savior.

As everyone sat quietly on the dirt floor, one Hindu man spoke in desperation at 11:50 p.m.: "If this Jesus Christ is Lord of all, then let Him send a man, woman, and boy flying from the sky to tell us that Jesus Christ is the Savior of the world." It was 11:55 p.m. when the Lord spoke to Brian, Sophia and Barry. At 12:10 am Brian, Sophia and Barry few down from the sky and into the concentration camp. At first, no one in the camp said anything; it was as if they were dreaming.

Brian spoke and said, "The Lord loves you." But again, no one understood his words. But then Barry spoke, and everyone's faces came alive, even the Christians. Barry spoke with a perfect dialect of modern Hindi. He told them how God had protected them when they were just little children. He walked over to a Hindu who was crippled and around 70 years old. To the awe of those present, Barry recounted how the man had fallen from a third story floor while working. "The Lord wants everyone to believe that He died for your sins. You don't have to keep being reincarnated over and over until you are

160

right with God. Jesus paid the price for your sins. He tasted death for everyone by being buried and going down to hell to take the keys of death from the enemy. Then on the third day, Jesus Christ rose to justify anyone who wants to come boldly to the throne of God. After you receive Jesus Christ as your savior by repenting of your sins, the Lord looks at the righteousness of Jesus Christ." The glory of God was on Barry's face as he spoke.

Though they had heard this message before, knowing they were going to be beheaded at noon the next day, everyone received what Brian was saying as Barry interpreted. Sophia started singing a song called "We're marching to Zion, that beautiful city of God." Barry interpreted the lyrics in Hindi, and Brian, Sophia and Barry sang in perfect harmony with everyone. Afterwards, Brian prayed while Barry translated. There was great joy in the hearts of all after hearing the message. Then Brian touched Sophia, and Sophia touched Barry, and they transported their bodies back to their home in the mountains. They did not get home until six in the morning. They went to bed feeling happy that so many people had given their souls to Jesus Christ.

After Barry had turned seven, every three days for the rest of that year, he and his parents were transported to Ethiopia, Ghana, Japan, Madagascar, Austria, New Zealand, The Russian Federation, and many other smaller countries. All of the miracles that had materialized in previous concentration camps also transpired in these former countries. But Brian, Sophia and Barry were growing tired of knowing that so many people were still going to die after they left the concentration camps. Russia was the last place they transported their bodies to win souls for Jesus Christ.

Chapter 38

It had been three days since the Lord had last called upon the family to do his work.

Growing restless, Sophia and Brian sat in their cave and began to discuss their situation. This was the first time they had found the time to talk about what was happening in the world since Barry had turned two.

"Why would The Lord allow so much evil to continue in the world Brian?" Sophia asked.

"Sophia, God doesn't so much allow evil, but rather he permits us to maintain our free will, even in the face of sinful choices. Mankind decided his own destiny when Adam and Eve fell from the Lord's grace. We wanted to be independent of the Lord. But once they did this, Satan had a door he could use to enter our lives here on earth. He was able to influence people through their free will, and even possess their minds, bodies, and souls. Sophia, why do you think the earth got so messed up?"

"Well, mankind polluted the air, the water, and the land." Sophia said.

"True, the Lord did not do this; the Lord did not pollute his own creation." Brian replied sleepily.

"But it was more than that Brian; there was something that changed in the very nature God had given us."

Brian nodded with a yawn: "At some point Sophia, human beings decided that they weren't going to live communally with the rest of God's creation anymore. We were tired of the hardships of the earth: the doubt, the helplessness, and the inconsistencies; and thereby decided that we were going to create our own world, one where we were in control. When we made this choice, we became our own gods."

"Brian, do you think those people could have foreseen that their choices would end up this way?"

"I don't know Sophia, but as we moved away from the Lord's design, the door was opened ever wider for Satan's influence."

To their surprise and joy, the Lord showed Himself to them then as they spoke about the problems of mankind. Barry was sleeping soundlessly between the two of them as God smiled at them and said, "It is as you have both said. Satan cannot do anything in this world unless he comes in illegally. His main purpose is to steal, kill and destroy everything that exists in harmony. However, I also did not have the right to come into this world unless I came through the door of human influence. The womb of a woman was that door. This is why I, the Christ, was born of a virgin. Once I became the second Adam, and gave my life for all fallen creatures, the whole of my creation was given a permanent second chance. Not only did I shed my blood to forgive all that had fallen from my grace, but I justified them when I rose from the dead. Therefore, whosoever faithfully receives my death will be saved if they believe in this message. I wanted humankind to understand that if they received the power of the Holy Ghost, they would have My kingdom living within them. My will was supposed to be on earth as it is in heaven." The Lord then showed Brian and Sophia the souls under the alter.

The Lord said, "They are crying out to Me to avenge them. I have told them they must wait until their brothers and sisters have been called back to join them."

Brian and Sophia looked at the Lord with reverence and said in unison, "Come Lord Jesus, come."

The Lord said, "It is going to be sooner than you think…just a few more souls. In the meantime, two of my great witnesses wish to meet the three of you before they are called back into my arms. Go now to Israel, and I will guide you." Then the Lord and His angels vanished.

Shortly thereafter, Brian, Sophia, and Barry transported their bodies to Israel, where they were able to meet the two witnesses. When they arrived, the three of them found themselves in a cozy little corner of a mud brick room, alone apart from two people sitting at a table. They had such a peace on their faces.

"Praise the Lord!" Brian, Sophia, and Barry said together when they saw the two witnesses seated before them.

The witnesses turned and looked at them with friendly smiles, saying, "Well, praise that wonderful name of Jesus." Everyone rejoiced and introduced themselves to each other.

After a moment, Brian said to them, "The Lord told us we would find you here."

The two witnesses nodded and asked the three of them, "Would you like to dine with us, and perhaps come to our home afterwards and have a visit?"

"We would love to," they all said.

Away from the restaurant, it was clear that the two witnesses lived deep underground. They had to hide from both the government and the much of the rest of world, as so many people wanted them killed. They were very powerful messengers; if they spoke something with the word of God, it would happen. Their speech was like a consuming fire. They all talked for hours of the goodness of the Lord and the hope of the future.

After a long period of silence, Barry said, "Who would ever have believed that the two of you would be those witnesses? The very ones the world thinks The Lord won't use will in the end have the greatest influence."

The witnesses smiled long and knowingly at the boy, but said nothing of his words.

Sophia smiled and agreed with her son, "The Lord told us that the ones who the world thinks are least capable are the very ones He would use to deliver his message. The two witnesses smiled. Even though they had the power to destroy cities when they spoke, they were filled with great compassion for the rest of humanity. They had the innocent spirits of children.

Looking serious for a moment, one of the witnesses spoke: "Things are getting worse, and we know that we will soon be killed by the people of this New Union; so we wanted to see the three of you before we died. We asked the Lord to

164

send you to us, and it is an honor to meet the three of you, especially you, Barry."

Barry laughed, "Me!?"

"Yes indeed, we saw you years before you were born little one. Now, don't any of you be discouraged, no matter what happens here in the near future? After all, it is the Lord who said, 'Look up, your redemption draws close.'"

And at that, they all made pleasant conversation until it began to get early, and the trio felt the call of the Lord to return to their mountain home. The next day, after Brian, Sophia, and Barry had met with the witnesses, they were both killed while preaching in Jerusalem. Their bodies lay in the streets for three days. After three days, at the Lord's command, they arose from the dead. At this, there was a great fear that came upon the world; the two of them could no longer be hurt or harmed by any means the humans had, nor could they be contained. Soon, the witnesses heard the Lord calling them to come home, and it came to pass that they were brought up to heaven. Since the media hadn't left their side since they had risen, many people witnessed this event on national television. After the witnesses ascended into heaven, Israel experienced a great earthquake, of a magnitude that had never before been felt in Israel or any part of the world.

Upon hearing this news, Sophia, Brian, and Barry were glad that the angels had warned them to leave the city beforehand. The three of them were now so weary.

They cried out to God. "Come Lord Jesus!"

After seven years of darkness, and seeing millions of Christians killed for the testimony of the Lord, many Israelites from all over the world took up the cross of Jesus Christ, wailing day and night for Him to come back and set up His kingdom. The more they witnessed for Jesus Christ, the more they too were killed. It seemed as if all of Israel would be destroyed like the Christians. There were very few Christians and Israelites left. The more The New Union killed the Israelites, the more zealously they witnessed for Jesus Christ, just as the first Disciples had done. The time of the gentiles was over. There was hardly any faith left within the gentile nations.

Only a few Christians that were left in concentration camps still had faith. Now the Jews were encouraging Christians to keep the faith, as the Lord Jesus was soon coming to set up His kingdom.

As the Lord sat with the angels, his voice was filled with pain: "I only wanted the best for my creation, even Satan. I gave them everything I knew would make them happy, yet I knew they would complain. I tried to win Lucifer's love by giving him a high seat above the other angels, hoping against hope that this would allow him to love me. But the more I gave him, the more he wanted. His first sin was thinking he was better than me, but his true crime was coming against My judgment. I waited and waited, and gave Satan space to repent. He took my mercy for granted though, and persuaded one-third of the angels to come against Me. Many were uncertain because I had not cast any judgment on Lucifer right away. They did not understand that I am a God of long-suffering. In truth, I knew Satan wasn't going to accept my goodness, but I wanted to give him a chance. In the end, I was forced to show My wrath. I was hurt that he hurt Me, but more so because he had turned so many angels against Me."

While the Lord spoke, He was in the form of Jesus Christ. The Lord paused for a while, and put his head down and wept. Several of the angels put their arms around Jesus to comfort Him. "Oh how I wish mankind would love me; I wish them good and not evil." The Lord not only felt pain for humankind but for all of the angels who had sinned against Him. The Lord was weeping with a loud wailing of the universe. The angels started to cry too. The Lord was shedding tears for all the creatures on the earth that were moaning for their creator to return and make things the way they were meant to be.

The Lord stopped crying then, and spoke to all of the angels and saints who had died throughout the ages: "It is time to pour my wrath out on the earth; I hear my people calling me. Get ready; Jesus Christ will now receive his bride, and pour out My judgment upon the earth. The Church will be taken out of the world, and will meet me in the air; We will land on the

Mount of Olives in Jerusalem. There is practically no faith left in the world now concerning the good news. The faithless have been destroying my earth, and have tried to destroy all the Christians. I must return now or no flesh will be left to be saved. I want some of the angels to separate those who are on My side from those who are not."

Then God told His army of saints and angels, a number that could not be numbered, to open the gates of heaven and leave for the earth. The angels blew the trumpets, and host was on its way. The earth fell under darkness, and the people could clearly see that the brightness that shown on Jesus Christ was great, as He came towards the earth on his flawless white horse. The multitudes that followed were indescribable. Though the sun had been scorching around 10 a.m.; now noon, the planet now was cold and black. But the warmth and brightness of Heaven was undeniable. The logic of mankind tried to reason it out with logic, as they did not want to believe the word of God. Humankind wanted to find their own explanation for the problems they were facing. If they had to follow the word of God, they would have to listen to what the Christians were teaching. Most people living in this moment did not want to believe the word of God.

Misguided and lost, the armies of the world pointed their long pointed tanks toward the sky. First, the dead in Christ were raised from their corruptible bodies, that the Lord could purify their flaws; and then their souls and spirits were placed in the new incorruptible vessels. The bodies in Christ that were still on the earth were similarly changed from corruptible to incorruptible. All were caught up together to meet the Lord in the air.

THE END...

"The Hidden Church... ReVealed"   All New - (2nd edition)

By Loretta Askew Owens

www.TheHiddenChurch.com and www.LorettaAskewOwens.com

Thank you, for your purchase.

For More Info about this Author and

our other Authors and Writers please visit our websites.

www.DNAeBooks.com and www.LorettaAskewOwens.com

"The Hidden Church... ReVealed" All New - (2nd edition)

By Loretta Askew Owens visit - www.TheHiddenChurch.com

Feel Free to Contact and Email Me: Loretta @DNAeBooks.com

Info@DNAeBooks.com

All Rights Reserved.

Including the rights NOT to reproduce this eBook,

Book or any portions thereof in any form whatsoever.

DNA eBooks Publishing Company

DNA eBooks Publishing Group

www.ingramcontent.com/pod-product-compliance
Lightning Source LLC
Chambersburg PA
CBHW070036260626
47159CB00005B/2056